THE SAXE POINT PARK MYSTERY

The Vancouver Island Mysteries Series, Volume 1

By P. N, Holland

Filidh Publishing

ISBN 978-1-927848-74-6
Filidh Publishing, Victoria, BC
Cover Design by Danny Weeds.
Cover Photography credits: iStockphoto ID: 859924224 Credit: alan64
iStockphoto ID: 907937690 Credit: fergregory and iStockphoto ID: 1500024964 Credit: Paolo Graziosi

Second Edition Copyright 2019 P.N. Holland
ISBN 978-0-2285-0214—2
First Choice Books, Victoria, BC
Original Copyright 2004 by P.N. Holland
ISBN 1-41204353-0
Independently published.

Also, by P.N. Holland
The Vancouver Island Mysteries Series:
The Lost Boys of Lampson, Volume 2
The E&N Escape, Volume 3
Vahldohr: Mellissadorha Series – Book One
Watch for more at https://pnholland.com/

****

To Ariel, Emily, and Zachary
who hopefully will enjoy my stories as they grow.

****

— CHAPTER ONE —

The Trunk

I could feel my tires bouncing over the roots in the trail as my old CCM, my cousin's old 'hand me down' bike, fenders rattling, flew over the branches from last night's wind storm. I knew I could keep up to Ricky if I didn't have Sarah behind me whining for us to wait up. She was so slow! Why did she have to follow me everywhere anyway? Weren't there girls who she could play with? But no, Mom had said that I had to watch her all summer. Some summer this would be, babysitting my noisy baby sister. "Ugh!"

In my haste and preoccupied with complaining, I missed a turn and was headed straight for a tree! I slammed on my foot brakes, but was too close and barely escaped by jumping off the bike and into a stand of choke cherry bushes beside the path. Ouch! Sarah, who was close behind me, hit my bike, which was in a crumpled heap in front of the tall fir tree. She fell off her bike and landed in a pile of brambles on the other side of the path. A flock of birds flew out of the bushes, screeching and scolding us.

"Help, Billy, get me out of here! They're picklies, and they hurt! Ow!" she howled at me. I yelled at Ricky, who was doubling back to see what was keeping us. He rammed on his brakes and hopped off of his new scarlet X-treme racer.

"What happened to you guys?" he said, surveying the scene of mangled metal, scraped knees and screaming child.

"What do you think? Billy forgot there was a tree in the path and ran into it, and I hit his stupid bike!" shrieked Sarah as she rubbed her sore knees, tears streaming down her cheeks.

"Sarah, it was an accident," I said in my defense. "My old bike doesn't corner fast enough. Here, let me help you out of the brambles." I offered as I reached down to pick her up out of the bushes.

"I don't need your help!" she scoffed, pushed me off and rose to her feet, yelping as she did when the prickles clung to her arms and legs. Both Ricky and I reached over anyway and pulled the clinging vines from her, freeing her at last. "I don't know why I have to follow you stupid boys around anyway!" she complained as we got on our bikes and headed down the path. Before we could answer her, Ricky shushed her and stopped us, saying he had spotted something suspicious over by the cove. We both asked what it was, and Ricky said he would show us, but we had to be quiet because he thought they might still be there. I had visions of pirates or gangsters or monsters in my head as we followed the path to the bank that overlooked the cove. The rocky beach hugged the shore in a semicircle which spread from a point of land to the west and trailed around south and east until it followed the rest of the shore and out of the cove. The trees along the bank blocked the sun and made the cove appear dark and foreboding. It was dusk, so the day was quickly receding, which gave the shadowy figures below an eerie appearance. We could see three men on the beach, and they were hauling something heavy up onto the logs and flotsam, which always hung around the rocky shore. The smell of seaweed wafted up to us, and crows cawed in the distance as they headed to the eastern trees to sleep for the night. The waves, gentle slapping against the rocks, sang their usual serenade to us as we neared the bank and peeked around the bushes to survey the cove below.

"I wonder what is in the crate," Ricky said what we were all thinking.

"Maybe it's buried treasure from some ship," Sarah said.

"Nah, more likely drugs like Marijuana or something." I countered. "The police have busted lots of ships trying to bring goods into B.C. along the shores around Vancouver Island. Smugglers trade drugs for them. I read that in the newspaper last week."

"We should go and tell the police," Ricky said.

"I know." I proposed, "Sarah, you go and tell Mom while we stay here and keep an eye on them in case they start to leave."

"No, I want to see too!" complained Sarah. I tried to talk her into going, but she wouldn't, and I wasn't about to start arguing with her while those men were only a short distance from us, so we all watched as the men moved the black crate closer to the path. We couldn't hear what they were saying, so I sneaked partway down the path, which was hidden by bushes and trees for most of the journey. As I crept closer, I could see a boat out in the cove. It looked like a small cabin cruiser about 16 feet in length with a row of lights in the middle. I couldn't tell the color as it was too dark, but there was someone inside flashing a flashlight beam at the three men. As I crept nearer to them, I could make out some of their conversation.

"...should have finished this by now. Come on, let's dump this and head back to town before the Coast Guard catches up with Cheryl." said one.

"Are you sure this is a safe place to hide this stuff, Ted?" asked another.

"Trust me; I grew up in this city. No one will ever think to look for it here," answered the one called Ted. "Now hurry up and help me haul this up the path to the van..." I wondered what place they were talking about. At that point, I realized that when they came up the path, they would see me, so I snuck back to Sarah and Ricky and told them that the men were coming and we had better hide.

"Let's hide over there behind the washrooms," whispered Ricky, pointing away from the cove toward a stone building over by the roadway.

"We'll have to hurry if we're going to get there before they reach the top of the bank," I whispered as I hopped on my broken bike and tried to ride it to the stone structure. It was not very rideable as my brake seemed crammed against my front tire, so I had to hop off of it and run with it along the path. Both Ricky and Sarah were making better headway than me, and I began to fear that I wouldn't make it on time. They rounded the corner of the building when I was still about ten meters away. Then Ricky whispered loudly for me to "drop!" and I jumped behind some bushes and pulled my bike behind me. I scraped my shin against a rock, and I felt a piercing pain go through it. I had to cover my mouth to keep from shouting, as I was not close enough to gain the safety of the building. My heart was in my throat, and I prayed that the men had not seen me. I heard voices coming along the path and peeked out to see if I was safely hidden from view. It was a good thing that I looked because my leg and back tire were both in plain sight. I quickly yanked my bike behind me and sat on my tire as I peered out between the brambles.

As they came nearer, I could see their faces and figures more clearly. The first one was the tallest, and he seemed to be the leader as the other two were carrying the crate. He had an old captain's hat on and a dark cape which made him look like an old seaman. Adding to this image was the pipe sticking out of his mouth that he seemed to be constantly puffing and causing rings of smoke to rise above him as he strode along. His two mates struggled along behind him with their heavy burden. The next one was a whole head smaller than the leader. He had light, flowing hair and a reddish beard. A cigarette was hanging off of his lip, and it looked like it had been there for quite some time because it was not lit and was stuck there. As he strained with the weight of the crate, he was pleading with the leader for a little rest. The captain started to complain about their schedule again but gave in and said to rest for five minutes. By this time, they were almost right in front of me as they set their burden down, and the two carrying it quickly sat on either end. The light-haired one with the beard pulled out a lighter and lit his stub of a cigarette. It was a wonder he didn't burn his beard off doing it! The man behind him was almost as tall as the leader with dark, wavy hair and a black mustache neatly trimmed into a thin line, and he stroked his thumb and first finger through it as he spoke.

"I'll be happy to part with this stuff and collect my money," he muttered.

"You and me both," agreed the small one with the red beard. "What did you say this was worth, Ted?"

"More than you will need for a long time, Charlie," Ted answered as he blew a ring of smoke from his pipe into the cool air.

“Why did that government guy in Seattle say that if anyone found out about this stuff, it would change the world?” questioned Sam, the man in the middle of the others.

“You don’t want to know! Trust me; this is bigger than all of us! Let’s just do this and get our money.” said Ted, quite agitated.

“Well, is the government looking for this stuff?” asked Sam, not willing to give up on this point.

“I don’t know, but the Americans have been touchy ever since “9-11,” and our contact in Seattle was pretty tight-lipped about it—wouldn’t even give us his real name.” continued Ted.

“Yeah, said his name was Michael Jackson, yeah right!” broke in Charlie.

They all laughed, and then the leader said that it was time to get moving again. His accomplices groaned and lifted their heavy load. As they did, the one with the cigarette stuck to his lip ran his tongue over it and spat it out in my direction, just missing my leg, which was resting awkwardly over my bike tire. I looked with distress toward my bike and noticed that the butt was smoldering in the brush behind me. Stupid idiot, I thought as I looked over to make sure that it was not starting a fire. I was careful not to kick my bike as I squashed my toe on it and watched with relief as they swiftly walked away toward the road. I glanced over to where Ricky and Sarah were standing beside the washroom, hidden from the view of the smugglers. They were both waving at me to catch up with them. I looked back toward the three thieves and saw that they had gained the roadway and were too far away to notice me, so I slowly rose, rubbed my cramped legs to help the circulation return, and then quickly walked my excuse for a bike up to where my friend and sister were.

“What did they say?” What did they have in that trunk?” they both shot at me at once.

“I don’t know what they were carrying, but it must be pretty important because they said that the American government was after them and that it could change the world!” I answered excitedly as I rubbed my sore leg.

“Wow!” they both responded.

"We'd better follow them!" Ricky said, his eyebrows raised.

"Wait!" I wailed as they both mounted their bikes. "I've got to put my chain back on and straighten my brake!"

"Okay, but hurry up, Billy, they're getting away!" whined Sarah.

"There, that should do it," I retorted as I wiped the grease from my chain on my jeans and mounted my rusty steed to follow them. My shin still ached, but the excitement of our quest made me quickly dismiss the pain. We just caught sight of them putting the case into the back of a black van. The parking lot was deserted, so it was easy to identify them as they scrambled into the front seat and began to drive away.

"We've got to follow them!" Ricky said urgently.

"Yes," I concurred, "Sarah, take out that pencil and paper you always carry and write down the license plate!" I commanded as I memorized the numbers.

T…A…N…The van whizzed past us, and I figured I'd catch the rest of the numbers from the back plate, but as it went past, I didn't see a rear plate! I asked Ricky if he got the numbers, and he said that he saw…T…A…N…2…but the others were covered in dirt and he couldn't read them. Sarah wrote down what we had and we headed after them. We just caught sight of them heading out of the park toward Flemings Beach. We sped as fast as our bikes would take us, but they steadily began to disappear ahead of us. Ricky, who had the fastest bike, was gaining ground as he sped ahead of us. After a few more turns, we lost sight of the van and Ricky. It wasn't until Sarah, and I reached Flemings Beach that we noticed Ricky had stopped at the top of the hill leading to the Army Barracks.

"Look, Ricky's up on the hill." I pointed. "They must have gone that way. Hurry, Sarah, let's follow him!" And with that, Sarah and I hopped back on our bikes and raced up the hill to the Army gate that led into the Barracks. When we met up with him, we stopped, and Ricky told us that the smugglers had headed toward the cove at the end of the road through the private married quarters or PMQs, as the military kids called them.

"Isn't there a marina down by the beach on the other side?" questioned Ricky. "Didn't we play pirates there just last week with Tommy and David Sanders?"

"Yah, the Bobbsey Twins," I recalled. We called them that because they were identical twins and we had all read the book.

"They must be planning on storing the crate somewhere over there," I added, putting two and two together.

"There's a shortcut through the PMQs. We can sneak over there by the Head Street entrance to the beach and walk around without being noticed," suggested Ricky.

"Let's go!" we all shouted at once. This had to be the first time that Sarah was excited about following us, and I was amazed at how well she kept up on her little bike; a little incentive goes a long way. In minutes, we were bouncing over the field and on the path between the hanger and the PMQs. As we flew by a group of kids along the pathway, I heard a couple of them call my name, but I just waved and peddled harder, not willing to stop and explain our hasty journey. They just stopped and stared until we were over the hill and then continued on their way, probably headed for Flemings Beach to beach comb and climb the cliff.

When we were at the Head Street entrance to the beach, it was getting a lot darker, and Sarah started to get worried about the time.

"What time is it, Billy?" she asked when we had dismounted our bikes.

"It's only nine o'clock, Sarah. We don't have to be home 'til nine-thirty," I reassured her as I glanced at my "Harry Potter" watch that I had received as a Christmas gift last year. She nodded her acceptance of my older brother's answer and looked toward the beach. It was hard to see far in the dim light, but the lights on the boats moored along the wharf to illuminate the bank for easy passage helped. We ditched our bikes under the stairs to the landing and headed along the beach toward the wharf that led to Pirate's Cove.

That's when Ricky sighted the black van parked along the roadway beside the plaque naming the historical site there. The men were not in the van, but we got the rest of the license plate by rubbing off the dirt. It was TAN 256. Sarah wrote the rest of the numbers on her "Harry Potter" notepad and said, "This should come in handy."

"Shh!" Ricky cautioned suddenly, "They're coming back. They were in that boat by the wharf." We looked carefully in the grey light and could see three men and a woman emerge from a sleek cabin cruiser that looked a lot like the one we saw at the cove in Saxe Point Park. We couldn't hear them, but we saw Ted, the leader, talk to the woman as the other two headed back toward the van. She went back inside the boat, and Ted followed his two companions up the stairs toward us.

"We'd better hide while they get into the van," I said, gesturing toward the trees on the other side of the road. We quickly ran across the road and hid behind a small copse of fir trees. We could see them get into the van, and when they drove off, we ran across to our bikes and attempted to follow. They turned up Head Street, and as we watched, peddling furiously, we noticed them turn right on Dunsmuir Road. We zoomed up the hill and followed onto Dunsmuir, hoping to see them, but they had disappeared.

"They could have gone left or right!" Ricky shouted, annoyed at not knowing which way to go as we approached Esquimalt Road.

"Go left on Wollaston, and I'll meet you at Head and Esquimalt!" I shouted up to him as I came to the intersection. "Sarah, you go back down Dunsmuir just in case we missed them." Sarah nodded and headed back along Dunsmuir as I peeled off to the left, up Esquimalt Road, hoping that if they came this way, they didn't go all the way back on Esquimalt or right up the hill. It was getting pretty dark, and hard to see any vans, let alone a black one, but we were determined. I slowed down at Head Street and looked carefully each way. Nothing looked like the van, but if they went into a garage, I could miss it and not even know it. As I looked down the street, I hoped that Ricky or Sarah had had better luck. I could see both of them waving at me at the end of Wollaston, so I headed down the hill and screeched my brakes to a stop as I reached them.

"Any luck?" Ricky asked in anticipation as Sarah looked on, her eyes wide.

"No, I was hoping one of you would have spotted it," I answered in disappointment.

"Nothing!" said Sarah with anger in her voice. "What time is it?" she asked with concern.

"Stop worrying," I told her, "It's only just past 9:30! We'll get home pretty quick."

"Bummer!" said Ricky, still thinking about the black van and his future as a secret agent. His favorite movies were all James Bond, and he had a set of toy weapons and secret service badges, gadgets and paraphernalia to rival Pierce Brosnan's. "We'd better get going then before our moms send out the police." He said sarcastically.

Sarah and I both looked at him with the same feeling of resigned disappointment and started to turn our bikes south to head down Head Street, when we both noticed the back of the black van streaking along Wollaston toward us. It hesitated for a second at the stop sign and then quickly crossed the street and headed east.

"Wait, Ricky," I shouted, "that looks like the van right there!" I pointed to the black van as it sped up the street.

Forgetting about the time, we hopped back on our bikes and followed the van, which had disappeared along Wollaston. When we reached the end of the street, we stopped and looked around.

"It could be anywhere," said Ricky, "maybe even further on into town."

"Well, let's look around here anyway," I said, in hopes of seeing something but beginning to worry about the time. "Mom and Dad get pretty steamed when we're late."

"We'd better get home now," said Sarah worried. "Come on, Billy! Remember last time we were late!"

"Hold it!" shouted Ricky. "Look over there!" He was pointing to the rear end of a black van sticking out of a driveway at the end of the street. The house looked like it was lost in time, with ivy-covered overhanging gables, an old wooden staircase and a tattered fence, almost completely swallowed up by bushes.

"Sarah, write down the address and then we'd better get home," I directed her as we looked at the small, dark house. I noticed that it was in pretty poor shape; the lawn hadn't been mowed for ages, the white picket fence in the front and sides was falling down, and the front porch screen door was partway off its hinges. It was dark, but it looked like it was in desperate need of a paint job as well. Sarah stuffed her notepad into her jeans, and we headed home down Dunsmuir Road toward Lampson Street. Once there, we zoomed south toward The Old England Inn and Greenwood Avenue, our street.

The streetlights were coming on, and cars had their headlights on. As they passed us, we couldn't help but feel that one of them would be our mom and dad's car with our parents angrily, anxiously looking for us. This made us peddle quickly but also left us with a feeling of impending doom as we got closer to our street. At the end of Greenwood, Ricky waved goodbye and peddled away from us, as he lived on Munro Avenue, down toward Flemings Beach. I shouted to him that I would call him tomorrow and we could investigate further. He waved and was gone.

"Well, Sarah, we'd better head home before we're any later," I said somberly.

"What time is it, Billy?" She looked very upset.

"It's just about 10:00 p.m." I answered, "Let's hurry!"

With that, we both jumped on our bikes and sped away down the hill. As we neared our house, I could see Mom on the front step looking out for us.

"Hi, Mom!" I waved and tried to sound like there was nothing wrong.

"You'd better get yourselves in here darn quick! We've been worried sick about you two! Young man, you're in trouble! It's way past 9:00 o'clock!" she shouted back at me.

I looked back at Sarah, who was starting to cry. I told her not to cry as it would only make it worse. She sniffled and stopped herself, wiped her eyes as she got off of her bike and walked it behind me into our garage.

"Sarah, don't say anything. I'll do the talking and take the blame, okay?" I tried to reassure her as we put our bikes against the wall. She just nodded her head, but I could tell that I hadn't convinced her that it was okay at all.

"Get up here, mister!" my dad shouted from the top of the basement stairs. I could feel my heart jump into my throat, and I began to shake. I hadn't had a spanking in a long time. A little late couldn't be that bad, could it? I slid my shoes off without undoing the laces and pulled my socks up. Sarah sat down to take off her shoes, and I slowly crawled up the stairs; my head hanging and my legs feeling like they had one-ton weights on them. Thump…thump…thump. Then I was at the top. I peered out toward the kitchen. I could see my father sitting at the table with my mother at the other end of it. They were talking quietly, but I could hear them.

"…The boys got to learn, Mary. He is so irresponsible!" My dad sounded angry, all right.

"He's only 10, Gerald. He has been looking after Sarah for half the summer already," pleaded my mom. She always tried to soften the blow. I was hoping she was succeeding, but my dad ruled the household and we all knew it.

"He's got to be punished, and that's all there is to it!" He yelled at all of us. I knew it was coming because my mom stopped talking and looked over to me and Sarah huddled at the entry to the kitchen. He looked at me with those cold, dark eyes, his forehead frowning, his cheeks red with anger. Here it comes. I could sense it as the seconds of torture ate me alive! I couldn't stand it, and I looked at the floor, hoping it would swallow me up and send me away, anywhere but here, a deserted island, the North Pole, the desert…

"Go to your rooms! Both of you! Get ready for bed and wait for me!" he thundered. We quickly turned and all but ran down the hall to our rooms. I could hear Sarah start to cry as she entered her room and began to wail through the wall. I couldn't cry anymore. I was 10 and had given up crying with my last spanking and had vowed not to cry ever again, no matter what. It was my secret pact with myself. I would be tough. I would show him I was tough. That's what he wanted, wasn't it? He would see. I could take it, any punishment. Of course, I was fooling myself, but I had no choice. I had to show him that I could take it.

My hands kept shaking as I got undressed. I put my shirt and jeans in the hamper at the end of the bed but kept my underwear on. Then I pulled my PJ's out from under my pillow and slid them on. I pulled off my socks and tossed them into the hamper, and said, *Two Points* to take my mind off the inevitable. I began to dream that I was on my secret agent rocket motorcycle chasing after a spy from Russia. He was in a Ferrari, squealing his tires around the corners, but he couldn't shake me. I was gaining on him. I could see his license and the rear guns from his bumper. Better not get too close. Just a little nearer and I could get him…a little closer…a little…

"You'd better be ready for bed, young man!" my father's voice shook me from my dream like a tiger shaking its prey. I looked up into his eyes as he opened my bedroom door. I began to shake again and felt hot; my heart was racing, my eyes watering. But I wasn't crying! No, sir, not me!

"Stand up!" my father shouted. I stood, and as I did, I could hear my sister moaning in the other room, waiting her turn…

- CHAPTER TWO -

The House

When I woke up the next morning, it was late. The sun was shining in, and I could hear the robins celebrating another beautiful day in Victoria. If it was so wonderful, why did I feel so awful? Oh yeah, last night…my father…my punishment…I could still feel it…

"Billy, time to get up!" I could hear my mom yelling at me from the kitchen.

"Yes, Mom!" I shouted back because I knew that if I didn't, she would come and make sure I was up. I got up, slid my PJ's off, threw them on the bed, grabbed my jeans from the floor, pulled them on and my "Radioactive" T-shirt, opened my drawer for a new pair of socks and sat down on my bed. As I yanked my socks on, I thought about how I was going to meet Ricky when Dad said that I was grounded for the rest of the week. E-mail, I guess.

"Hurry up. Breakfast is ready, and it's getting cold," that was my mom again making sure I got fed.

"Right there!" I replied, as I picked up my brush from the dresser and attempted to make myself look human. I looked like I hadn't slept. I felt like I hadn't slept. Then I remembered a dream I had last night; something about other worlds and inter-dimensional portholes in the fabric of time. I was a traveler to other dimensions through a secret passage created by a time and dimension-bending machine that a physicist had developed. I was in Zacon, a world where dinosaur-like creatures that looked like raptors controlled society and mammals like us were kept as pets. It was scary and…

"Billy, come and get your breakfast before I feed it to Rasputin!" my mother's voice broke through the time barrier, and I returned to planet Earth promptly. Besides, I was hungry, and Rasputin had already eaten enough of my meals when I was late for them. It had been a long time since dinner last night, and I hadn't eaten much. I quickly left my room and headed for the kitchen, where my sister Sarah was already devouring eggs, orange juice and toast with marmalade. It is beyond me how she eats so much and remains skinny as a rake, but she does. I guess it's because we never stop doing stuff, and we're always on the go. That's why this grounding is going to be so tough to take. I sat quietly in my place, and Rasputin moved sneakily to my side under the table as I was a much better provider than my sister. I could feel his muzzle up against my leg, and I lightly patted his head and floppy ears. His cocker spaniel breath felt warm against my fingers as he checked them for food.

"Don't you feed that mutt, Billy. He's getting too fat on scraps, and he's already had his breakfast." Mother lectured. *I'm sure it wasn't what he ordered,* I thought to myself. My eggs and toast smelled good, and I was hungry. I picked up my toast and spread butter and strawberry jam on it. It was gone in seconds, everything that was except the crusts; I don't eat crusts. That's where Rasputin comes in, I quietly put my crust down on my leg, and he snapped it up and gulped it. I thought we were in the clear because Mom was doing dishes, facing the window, but Sarah was watching.

"Mom, Billy is feeding the dog again," she squealed. I gave her a look of contempt, and she smiled at me. I guess she was paying me back for getting her into trouble last night.

"Billy, what have I told you about feeding that beast!" she turned and glared at me.

I rolled my eyes, "I know he is getting overweight and needs a diet. Why don't we give him your "Juice Plus" pills?"

"Don't get smart, young man." She retorted, trying to look cross, but I could tell she was trying to keep from laughing, and Sarah was snickering under her breath. At least Mom had a sense of humor. My dad would freak out and tell me not to be insolent.

"Sorry, Mom," I replied with a smile back at my sister, who was still snickering and didn't seem to care about pushing the point. Meanwhile, Rasputin was sniffing frantically at my leg, looking for more food. I patted him on the head and continued with my breakfast.

"Mom, do we have to stay in all day?" Sarah whined.

"That's what your father said," Mom dismissed her.

"It's not fair if you ask me." I chimed in.

"Well, you should have thought of that before you came home late a second time this week." Mom reminded us.

"Can I use the computer?" I asked, "And the phone?"

"I suppose so, but you have to clean up that room first," she answered, using the opportunity to get me to do something that I hadn't done in a week.

"But it's not Saturday?" I complained.

"Do you want to use the computer or not?" was the response, and I realized, like all children, that life was not fair, and I had better not push my luck, even with Mom. She may be the easy one, but she would only take so much, and then she'd get angry too. With no more leeway to bargain with, I resigned myself to cleaning my room first.

"Okay, okay, Mom, I get the point." I shrugged.

"What about me, Mom?" asked Sarah, hopefully.

"Same deal." was the quick response. Again, I smiled at her to let her know that she had not won either. She began to pout but thought better of it, I guess, as she just smiled back at me and then continued to eat. I finished up my eggs and toast, slyly fed the crusts to Rasputin and stood up to take my dishes over to the sink.

"I'm going to clean my room now, okay, Mom?" I sang as I left the table.

"Okay, dear." Was the quiet response as I handed her my dirty dishes. "Oh, and honey, could you please pick up your clothes and take them downstairs so that I can start the laundry before I leave? Thanks, dear." she continued before I could answer. Mom worked part-time in a lawyer's office and didn't have to be in until II: 00a.m. on Wednesdays. As she wiped her hands dry, she turned to my sister and told her to finish drying and putting away the dishes because she was running a little late and needed to get ready for work. I glanced up at the clock above the stove and saw that it was almost 10:30 already. *I better phone Ricky*, I thought, just as the phone rang.

"I'll get it!" I hollered at my mom and grabbed the portable receiver off of its cradle in the hall as I passed on my way to my room. "Hello? Oh, hi Ricky."

"Man, you sure slept late this morning," he answered.

"It's worse than that! I'm grounded!" I complained.

"Bummer!" he reacted, "Maybe you could get out of it if you talked to your mom."

"I don't think so, but I'll try," I responded with little hope.

"Anyway, listen; I found out something pretty interesting. You remember when you said that the government was looking for these guys?" he said excitedly.

"Yeah, so?" I encouraged.

"Well, my dad is a cop, right?" he prompted.

"Yeah, so?" I persisted, "Tell me what you're getting at!"

"I overheard him this morning, and he was talking on the phone to someone about stolen secrets!"

"Did you tell him about what we know?" I asked, getting more excited as we spoke.

"I didn't have a chance; he was out the door before I was up. I tried to tell my mom, but she says that I'm imagining things and I should be careful where I'm going and who I'm spying on." Rickyy answered, discouraged.

"We've got to go and check out that old house!" I said.

"I know, but you're grounded," said Ricky with dismay.

"Leave that to me, Ricky. I'll call you back when my mom's gone, okay?" I said, with the question of how I was going to pull this off already buzzing around in my head. Just as I put the receiver down, Mom came down the stairs from her bedroom.

"Who was on the phone, dear?" she said as she tried to put on her left earring.

"Just Ricky, Mom," I responded.

"You know you're grounded." She reminded me, anticipating my thoughts.

"Yes, Mom, but if I clean my room, can't I go out just for a little while? Long before dad comes home." I assured her.

"Well, if your room is done and you must mind your sister and be home by 3:00 p.m., I'll phone, and if you're not here, you'll be grounded for a month!" she threatened.

"I will, I promise, Mom!" I gave her a big hug.

"Never mind the sucking up! You just make sure this time!" she said firmly, but she did hug me back, and that felt good. I loved my mom! Then she pranced into the hall, her heels clattering on the tiles, put on her coat and called Sarah. Sarah came bounding out of the kitchen with marmalade still tattooed on her face and sticky fingers.

"Yes, Mom?"

"You finish those dishes, clean your room and mind your brother! Both of you had better be back in this house by 3:00 p.m., or there will be Hell to pay! Do you understand?" she shook her finger at Sarah, put her hands on her hips and turned to face me.

"Make sure you lock up when you leave!"

"Yes, mam!" I saluted. Then she turned on her heel, grabbed her purse from the hall table and headed out the basement door.

"Thanks again, Mom!" I called as she descended the stairs. Sarah was licking her fingers and looked at me with curiosity in her eyes.

"What did Ricky say?" she questioned.

"I'll tell you later, Sarah. Right now, you have to finish the dishes, and we have to clean our rooms. Then I'll tell you everything." I tried to get her moving and pushed her toward the kitchen.

"I'm going, I'm going!" she whined at me as she slowly sauntered down the hall. I turned and headed for my bedroom. Then I remembered I had to call Ricky. I reached back for the phone in the hall and dialed his number.

"Hello?" It was Ricky.

"Hi, Ricky, it's Billy. We have to clean our rooms, and then I'll call you when we're ready to leave, okay?" I said.

"Alright, I'll be waiting," he replied. I hung up the receiver and headed back toward my bedroom.

--*-*-*

After half an hour, my bedroom looked the cleanest it had been in months. I even did my "Harry Potter" sheets and blankets hospital style. At least that's what mom calls it when the corners are tight, and the pillow is covered with the comforter. My stuffed dinosaurs and military men were poised, ready for battle, on top of my shelf, and my dresser was clear with my clean clothes neatly sorted and folded inside. My closet was neat, with my Disney game and Star Wars on the shelves. My computer was clear, and all my games for it were stacked underneath. I just hoped that nobody would look under the bed. Oh, well, it was pretty good. It would do. I left my room and headed for Sarah's room. I better get her going, or we will never get out of here. I knocked on her door.

"Come in!" she bellowed. When I entered, I was shocked. Her clothes were all over the floor, books piled on her chair, and Barbies were in various states of disarray on her dresser, the floor, and her bed. She was lying there looking at a magazine or Archie comic; I couldn't tell.

"Sarah, come on! You've got to clean it up, or we'll never get out of here!" I complained.

"So?" she nonchalantly waved at me in between her pages of comedy.

"Don't you want to go and see what's in that house?" I responded in exasperation.

"Maybe," she casually replied while wiping hair from her eyes.

"Look, I'll help you clean your room. Okay?" I offered.

"Okay," she answered noncommittally. Slowly she rose from her story and sat on the bed. I quickly began picking up toys, cards and Barbies and tossed them into her toy box at the foot of the bed.

"Hey, don't throw my stuff!" she complained.

"Then help me put them away!" I countered. With that, she began to pick stuff up and put it where it belonged. It took us another half hour to finish her room. When I looked at my watch, I noticed that it was already 12:00 p.m.

"What time is it?" Sarah asked.

"Just gone 12:00 p.m.," I answered.

"I'm hungry; it's lunchtime," she squealed. I'm never going to get out of here! I thought.

"Look, we'll grab an apple on the way out, okay? We don't have time for a full meal," I suggested frustration in my voice.

"That's not a lunch!" Sarah complained.

"How about some cookies with it?" I said, my frustration level getting higher by the minute.

"Okay," she agreed, "but I want three of them, and they have to be the chocolate ones. I don't like the coconut ones."

"Okay, okay, okay!" I yelled as I ran for the kitchen to get the goodies. Finally, we were ready. It was 12:10! I had my backpack on with cookies, water, apples and my walkie-talkies in it. As we headed toward the basement door, I picked up the phone and dialed Ricky.

"Hello?" he answered.

"Hi, Ricky, we're leaving now. We'll meet you at the top of Greenwood, okay?" I quickly stated.

"Sounds good; see you in a bit." He agreed and hung up the phone. I hung up, too and Sarah and I headed down the stairs toward our bikes. I made sure that I locked the garage door behind us, and we were on our way. When we reached the top of Greenwood, we could see Ricky coming up Lampson Street. He put on his brakes and stopped at our street.

"Ricky, tell Sarah what you told me this morning," I suggested.

"Okay," he started, "I overheard my dad talking about a government agent who had heard about some stolen secret documents that the US authorities were pretty upset about."

"Did they say anything about robbers?" asked Sarah.

"No, but my dad was pretty sure they had smuggled something into Canada because I heard him say stuff like smugglers and Coast Guard and secret documents and stuff like that." continued Ricky.

"Wow!" both Sarah and I said at once.

"We'd better go and check out that house!" I said.

"Yeah, let's go!" agreed Ricky, and he headed up Lampson with Sarah and myself close behind. When we reached Wollaston, I glanced at my watch. It was 12:25. We only had two hours to investigate before we had to head for home again. We should have been earlier last night, I thought.

Ricky was the first to reach the old house at the end of the block. It looked desolate and gloomy, even in the sunshine! There was no van in the driveway, and the windows were dark with the curtains drawn, like a funeral home. The high unkempt bushes crept all the way up to the front porch and sat there like some hungry guest, ready to swallow the stairs. The rest of the house waited patiently for the same fate as heavy blackberry bushes, overhanging trees, and cedar shrubbery scratched against the walls and roof like gruesome dinner ghouls scraping their knives and forks. As we dropped our bikes and slowly stepped forward, a cold wind blew down from the old chimney on the roof, making me shiver in my t-shirt. How could that happen on a warm summer day when the weatherman had said that the day's high was expected to be around 30 degrees. I could see Sarah's hair whip about her face as she whimpered.

"Billy, I don't think this is such a good idea."

"Don't worry. There's nothing here! You'll be safe." I replied, more trying to convince myself than my sister.

"Yeah, It's probably just a gust of wind from the water." piped in Ricky. "We get 'em all of the time down by Flemings Beach." None of us seemed relieved by our thoughts, but we slowly continued up the walkway to the front porch. As Ricky stepped on the old boards, they creaked and complained. He stopped, turned and looked back at us in surprise.

"Just old warped wood," I said, trying to take away our fear.

"Yeah, they probably should have torn this old relic down years ago," added Ricky.

Sarah and I stood on the steps watching as Ricky tiptoed to the front door. He carefully reached forward and tried the door knob, which looked like something out of "Alice in Wonderland." It would not budge. He tried again, then turned and said, "Well, I guess we aren't getting in that way."

"Let's see if any windows are open," I suggested as I descended the stairs and headed around the side of the house along a narrow path between the trees and the blackberry brambles. The wind stirred the leaves and branches, and I could hear an eerie scraping against one of the windows. Sarah hesitantly followed me with Ricky in the rear. Around the side of the derelict relic were two windows at ground level. I pushed past the blackberries, scratching my legs and peered into the closest one. It looked like it entered into a basement, as I could see walls and an old workbench. On top of the bench, I thought I could see the trunk that the smugglers were carrying yesterday. I couldn't be sure because of the darkness.

"Hey, Ricky, I think I can see the old trunk we saw in the park yesterday!" I shouted with excitement.

"Really?" he queried, "Let me see!" and he pushed past Sarah to get a look into the window. I stepped back, and as I did, Sarah accidentally fell into the blackberry brambles along the path.

"Billy!" she screamed, "You pushed me into the pricklies!"

"Sorry, Sarah," I offered to help her out and tried not to giggle at her predicament. She swatted my hand away and angrily stated that she could get out by herself; thank you! So, I turned and asked Ricky if he could see the trunk.

"I'm not sure. It's too dark!" came the reply. "I wonder if there is a way inside." As he spoke, I was already moving around toward the back of the house to see if there was another door. Sarah had successfully extracted herself from the "pricklies" and was following me. I stopped in front of the back door, which was not in good shape. In fact, there was a hole at the bottom of it which ended in the dirt underneath as if some animal had been burrowing to get inside. I reached down on my hands and knees, felt around the hole and noticed a cold draft coming from inside. It sent a chill through me, and I quickly stood up again. Sarah saw me shiver and asked what was wrong. Then she reached down too.

"Why is there a draft coming from the inside?" I asked nobody in particular.

"Weird!" said Ricky. "Can you crawl through that hole?"

"No," I replied, both in frustration and relief, as I didn't want to go into that cold, drafty place.

"But I can." It was Sarah. The next thing I realized was that she had already got her head and shoulders through the small opening. As Ricky and I watched in amazement, she disappeared under the door. A second later, we heard a latch give way from the other side, and the door swung open with a whoosh! A proud Sarah was standing there before us with her arms folded.

"Sarah, super sleuth!" she announced. We both laughed and proceeded inside the old house. As soon as I crossed that uninviting threshold, I felt uneasy. I didn't want to continue, but something urged me forward. Curiosity? Adventure? Was it like in the Harry Potter movie when they opened the secret door to "The Chamber of Secrets"? The cold, dank air seemed to be saying, "Leave before it is too late!" Then Ricky tripped over something and went sprawling over Sarah, who screamed that something knocked her over, and it was organized chaos.

"Help! Something grabbed me!" wailed Sarah.

"Oof!" Ricky moaned as he tumbled over Sarah.

"Sarah, it's only Ricky. He's bumped into you. Stop screaming. You'll wake the dead!" I scolded.

"Oh!" groaned Sarah.

"Sorry!" Ricky apologized, "I fell over something in the dark. Hold it. I have a flashlight. Just let me fetch it out of my pocket." He rummaged around in his pants pocket and brought out one of those small mega lights, and turned it on. As he scanned the room, we all looked around. We could see the walls with ropes, cords and tools hanging from them. There were old jackets, pants and shirts on hooks hanging in a makeshift closet under the stairs that led upstairs. Old machines like drill presses, table saws, and different lathes stood under and alongside the bench. And on the bench was the trunk. It was the same one that we saw at Saxe Point Park!

"Look!" I shouted. "There is the trunk!"

"I wonder what's in it!" Ricky chimed in as we headed toward it.

"Be careful!" cautioned Sarah. "We don't know what is in it. It might be dangerous!" We stood in front of the old trunk for a minute, excitement and indecision on our faces. Should we open it? What if it is dangerous? There is nobody else here to help us. I'm sure we were all thinking the same things.

Finally, Ricky spoke. "Maybe only one of us should open it while the others stay at a safe distance. That way, if something happens, the others could go and get help." He reasoned.

"Sounds good, Ricky, but who opens it?" I countered.

"Not me!" said Sarah, definitely.

"Why not? You seemed courageous enough when you went through that hole in the door!" I argued.

"That was different. We looked through the window and knew there was nobody in the house. It wasn't scary!" she replied.

"I know!" said Ricky suddenly. "We'll draw straws. I saw it in a movie, and it was chance instead of choice."

"Sounds fair," I agreed.

"Okay," Sarah said meekly. So, we looked around for something to use as straws. Over by the staircase, I found an old straw broom and brought it over to the bench. Carefully, Ricky broke off six straws, making sure one of them was shorter than the rest and wrapped them in a cloth he had found so that only the ends were showing. He mixed them around so none of us would know which one was shorter than the rest.

"We'll draw until one of us pulls the short one." He announced. I went first. Gingerly reaching forward, I pulled one right in the middle. It was a long one. I sighed in relief. Next, Sarah pulled one out really slowly. It was also a long one. Ricky breathed in deeply and pulled one out with his left hand. It was a long one too. We all sighed and looked at the straws left. There were only three now. I started to pull on the one nearest to me when it came out real quick. It was the short one! I stood there for a moment, looking at Ricky and Sarah and them staring at me. We all turned and looked at the closed trunk.

"Oh, well, probably full of mothballs anyway." I laughed. Sarah and Ricky laughed with me. I slowly stepped forward, imagining myself as "Harry Potter creeping into the spider's cave in the enchanted forest." Ricky and Sarah moved back toward the door. Ready to run!

The trunk had a seal or crest on the top of it that I hadn't noticed before. "Hey, guys, there's writing on the top of it," I explained.

"What does it say?" they both answered at once.

"It's hard to make out. I think it says USAF 51 03 02 21 MAGESTIC," I read as I dusted off the lettering with my fingers.

"I wonder what that means." Ricky echoed my thoughts.

"Sounds Top Secret, all right!" Sarah said, reminding us of Ricky's dad's words about smugglers, Coast Guard and government…etc.

"I'm going to open it now," I stated, although it sounded more like a question. My hands were clammy, and my heart was pounding as I reached for the clasp on the old trunk. But, hold on; it was locked with a big padlock.

"Ah, guys, there is a big padlock on this thing," I stated with more relief than disappointment.

"What?" they both whined.

"We need a key." I offered.

"Fat chance of finding that here," Ricky said in disbelief.

"Wouldn't you know it? We get this close, and we're stopped by a stupid key!" Just then, we heard a door slam upstairs.

- CHAPTER THREE -

Kidnapped

"Oh, no!" Sarah hissed. "Somebody is here!"

"They've come back!" Ricky said. "Quick, let's hide!" At that, we looked around for a place to hide. Sarah noticed a couple of wooden crates against the back wall, away from the windows, with nothing behind them.

"Hey, you guys, we can hide behind these. They're quite big." She stated as she glanced behind one of them. We scrambled over behind them and crouched down with our eyes peering through the slates. In a couple of seconds, we could hear footsteps on the staircase. My heart felt like it was in my mouth as I strained to see who was coming down the stairs. I could just make out a tall figure and a smaller person following. The one in front had a flashlight. He was looking for something on the wall. It was a switch which suddenly lit a light bulb over the bench hanging from the ceiling. I could see more clearly now. It was the one who looked like a sea captain with the same black cape and pipe in his mouth. The smaller one, though, was a woman. She was speaking to him as he reached for something in his pocket.

"Ted, we only have a few days to unload this thing. It's making me nervous having it here. What if someone finds it? Breaks in…" she whined.

"You worry too much. Nobody is interested in an old house like this. That's why this place was so perfect. Good thing Mom never sold it years ago. We'll have this unloaded by the end of the week." He stated. As he said this, he took what looked like a key out of his pocket and undid the padlock. The lock snapped as it released, and he pulled it from the latch, placing it on the bench.

"I'll be glad when this is over." The woman continued to complain. The man ignored her and lifted the lid. We held our breath as we watched, not knowing what to expect. There was no explosion, nobody disappeared, nothing happened. We did see, however, the man lift something heavy from the trunk. It appeared to have lights on it and was shaped like a helmet, a very shiny one. He placed it carefully on the bench and caught his breath.

"What did you say that thing was worth?" the woman questioned.

"More than a few million; at least, that's what that agent from Seattle told me," answered Ted.

"We could do a lot with that money, baby." added the woman, "But what about those other guys?"

"Don't worry about them. I'll take care of them when the time is right." Ted answered with a snicker.

"Where are they now?" she continued.

"I sent them to contact the buyer. He's in town, and I want him to give us a time and place to meet." Ted explained.

"Why didn't you go yourself?" the woman asked.

"This way, Cheryl, they don't meet me and know what I look like. It's safer for us," he answered as he hugged her.

She responded by kissing him on the cheek. "You're so smart, Ted. You've thought of everything."

"Of course, baby," he answered with a sly smile. "We'd better put that thing back in the trunk for safekeeping." He reached over Cheryl to pick it up.

"Hold on," she stopped him, "I want to try it before you put it away."

"No!" countered Ted, "It's too dangerous! The last person who did that without knowing how to control it disappeared and hasn't been heard from since!" At this comment, we looked at each other in disbelief.

"I thought you said the directions were here too?" whined Cheryl.

"Yes, but it's more than just directions. You have to be trained properly. The agent in Seattle warned me about using it without a guide. Look, let's just put it away for now. Those other guys should be back any minute with the details of our meet." Ted reasoned with Cheryl, who took her hand off of the helmet and let him put it back in the trunk with the other things in there. The kids watched in fascination. They could see another machine of some sort and what looked like a weapon or a wand of some kind with a red crystal at one end.

"Come on, let's go back upstairs for a drink while we wait for the others," suggested Ted, as he closed and padlocked the trunk. Cheryl had turned and was leading the way up the stairs as Ted reached over to the wall and hit the light switch. When their steps were not heard anymore, we came out from behind the crates and approached the back door.

"Wow! Did you see what was in that trunk?" whispered Ricky.

"Yeah! I wonder what happens when you put that helmet on." I whispered back.

"We have to get out of here before those other guys get back. What time is it, Billy?" asked Sarah.

"It's 2:30! We had better get going. If we're late again, Mom is going to ground us for a month!" I whispered harshly.

"Okay," agreed Ricky, and we headed quietly out the back door of the house. He led the way with me next and Sarah bringing up the rear as usual. As we cornered the house toward the side hedges, Ricky suddenly stopped us short.

"Hold it! Someone's coming up the front pathway. Quick, hide in the hedge!" he warned. We scampered into the blackberry-infested hedge and peered out between the bushes. Sarah started to complain about prickle bushes.

"Quiet, Sarah, they might hear you." I softly whispered in her ear. As I looked out again toward the house, I saw two men climbing the stairs to the front porch. I recognized them as Charlie and Sam, the other two smugglers. Once they had entered the house, we scurried out of the bushes and over to our bikes which we had ditched by the rickety fence. Catching our breath, we quickly mounted our bikes and headed down Wollaston toward Lampson Street. As we left, I glanced back at the house and thought I saw one of the smugglers looking out of a window, which faced Wollaston.

"When we get home, I'm going to call the police!" I shouted at Sarah and Ricky.

"Yeah, but they probably won't listen. I talk to my dad all the time, and he says that I just imagine things. Parents don't take us seriously. They're too full of their jobs and stuff to pay us much attention." Ricky doubted.

"Well, I'm going to try. I think one of them saw us leaving, and anyway, this is too important to just let go!" I shouted back.

"Well, good luck with that. Let me know if they believe you!" Ricky shouted back. "Are you sure one of them saw us?" he questioned.

"I don't know, but we had better peddle hard, just in case!" I yelled back.

"Anyway, I have to get home too 'cause my mom wants to take me to the dentist today. Yuck! I think I've got a cavity. See you guys later!" he hollered as he headed down Lampson ahead of us.

"Okay! Good luck at the dentist!" we both shouted back at him.

"Come on, Sarah!" I yelled, "We'd better get moving and get home before Mom calls!"

"Right behind you, Billy!" she shouted as we headed up Lyall Street and then on to Joffrey. As we rounded the corner to Kinver, a black van sped by us and just about ran us over.

"Hey, watch it!" I shouted but quickly shut up when I noticed the license plate. TAN 256! "Sarah! Stop!" I screamed.

"What!" she wailed as she just about ran into my bike, hit her brakes and screeched to a halt.

"That van!" I pointed, "It's the black van! Hurry!" I hopped back on my rickety old bike and raced ahead down Kinver and past Wychbury Street without even stopping at the stop sign! Luckily no cars were coming.

"There go the smugglers!" I yelled again.

"Did they see us?" she wailed. "Billy, I'm scared!"

"I don't know, but we'd better get home fast before they decide to turn around." I tried to sound confident, but my heart was pounding, and my hands felt clammy again.

We both jumped back on our bikes and headed down Wychbury instead of Greenwood, just in case they were watching. That way, they would think we lived on a different street. We peddled hard, constantly looking back to see if we were being followed, but no black van appeared. When we reached the back of our house, we crossed through the neighbor's gate to get to our backyard and safety. We dropped our bikes and ran for the back door. I dropped my key in my haste and had to go on hands and knees to try and find it. Sarah dropped, too and helped me look for it.

"Darn it! What a stupid time to lose the key! Help me, Sarah; Mom is going to be calling any minute!" I whined in desperation. Just then, I could hear our phone ringing.

"Oh, no! That's Mom now!" screeched Sarah. "Come on, Billy, it's got to be here somewhere!" But the grass was too thick to find it. Finally, we gave up and slumped down on the grass in a miserable heap. Sarah began to whimper, and I looked to the blue sky, but it offered no help. I could still hear the phone ring, and I drifted into dreamland, wishing I was a million kilometers away in some exotic country— a spy hunting down that mysterious evil agent, Vladimir Pushkin, the scourge of the Russian mafia.

"What are we going to do now?" Sarah broke my daydream, and I looked over at her and then over to the back of the house. I saw our ladder attached to the back deck, and my window was open.

"I know. We'll use the ladder, and I can climb in my bedroom window! Quick, help me, Sarah!" I shouted as I heard the last ring of our telephone, and then it was quiet again.

"But what if the neighbors see us? They might call the cops!" Sarah argued.

"We have to take that chance, Sarah. If I can get inside, I can call Mom back and explain that I lost the key and we had to climb in through the window. Maybe she won't be so mad. It's the only chance we have!" I pulled her up by the arm, and we both headed toward the ladder. Unfortunately, it was high up on two hooks attached to the side of the back deck.

"Sarah, I'm going to have to boost you up so that you can reach the ladder and unhook the latches, okay?" I suggested.

"I don't know, Billy, it might fall on us." she hesitated.

"We've got to try it!" I attempted to convince her.

"Okay, but if it falls…" she trailed off as I hoisted her up against the siding of the deck. Slowly she raised herself higher and higher, and finally, she could just reach the ladder's runners. She carefully pushed the ladder upwards until it was free from its hook. She gently lowered it but let go halfway down because I lost my footing, and she and the ladder fell on top of me onto the grass below.

"Oof!" I yelped as I fell over, and Sarah screamed. We ended up in a tangled heap with the end of the ladder over our backs. The runner had struck Sarah in the head, and she was now whimpering in pain. I pushed the ladder off of us and asked her if she was okay. She responded by rubbing her head and declaring that none of this would have happened if I hadn't been such a klutz and lost the key in the first place. I agreed and told her I was sorry as I helped her up. She shook me off and grimaced in pain, but she was okay.

"Help me pull the ladder off the other hook, Sarah, and we can hoist it up to my window," I directed.

"Oh, alright." she groaned, still angry from the mishap. We carefully released the other end of the ladder and let it drop to the lawn. Then we carried it to my window, and both holding the runners, hoisted it against my window ledge. I carefully tested the first rung and told Sarah to hold the bottom of the ladder much the same way Dad had taught me when he went up ladders. She obliged begrudgingly, and I started my ascent. I was a little shaky but finally reached my window ledge, pulled my window wide open by pushing it inside the channel as far as I could, stepped up one more rung and gently fell head-first into my bedroom. Luckily, I landed on my bed which was situated underneath the window, as I liked fresh air when I slept. I quickly turned around, looked out the window and called to Sarah that I was in. She left the ladder and headed for the back basement door.

I ran downstairs; glancing at the phone and answering machine on the hall desk, I noticed that there was a message. As I hit the stairs, I could hear Rasputin barking. I ran into him as I rounded the door to the rec room. I patted him and kept on running as he wagged his tail. When I came back up with Sarah, I listened to the message. It was from Mom "…Billy, where are you and Sarah! You had better have a good explanation, or you're grounded for a week! Phone me back a.s.a.p!" I knew my mom was ticked, but I was sure she would understand. I dialed her number…

"Hello, this is Billy Maclean. Is my mom there, please?" I asked.

"Oh, hi Billy, this is Leanne. Hold on. I'll get your mom."

The receptionist said sweetly. I held on with bated breath, worried about what Mom would say. My hands started shaking again as I heard Mom's footsteps on the office tile coming toward the phone.

"Billy, where were you two?" she said sternly.

"We were in the backyard, Mom, just coming home, but I lost my key in the grass, and we couldn't get in, so I had to climb the ladder and come through my bedroom window, and by the time I did that, you had hung up," I explained, out of breath.

"Oh. Well, you had better go back out there and find that key before your father gets home. And by the way, take out some chicken for supper tonight." she answered calmly.

"You mean we're not grounded?" I said hopefully while Sarah rolled her eyes at me, still mad about the lost key and her sore head.

"No, but you had better find that key!" Mom ordered, and then she put the receiver down rather hard.

"I think she's a little mad, but we're not grounded, Sarah!" I said as I hung up the phone.

"No thanks to you, Billy!" she groaned as she continued to rub her head. " I've got a headache because of you!"

"I'm sorry, Sarah, but it was an accident." I consoled her. "Do you want me to get you some Tylenol?" I suggested.

"No, I'll be okay, I guess," she said uncertainly. "We'd better go get that key before something else happens." With that, we both headed down the stairs and out the back door, being careful not to let Rasputin out. We put the ladder over by the deck, and I got a chair from the basement so that I could reach the hooks to put it away. After we had done that, we started looking for the lost key. I was thinking that I should have mowed the lawn last week just as I heard the phone ring. I told Sarah to keep looking, and I rushed inside to get the phone. After the third ring, I picked up the receiver. It was Ricky.

"Billy, I talked to my dad about the house and the stolen stuff, and he said he was going to investigate!" he said excitedly.

"Wow, that's great!" I replied.

"Yeah," Ricky went on, "I told him about the black van, too, but I couldn't remember the license plate. Do you remember?"

"No, but Sarah wrote it down on her Harry Potter notepad. I'll go ask her, then phone you back, okay?" I answered.

"Alright, talk to you later," Ricky said and hung up. As I walked back downstairs, I was thinking how relieved I was now that the police were involved. I was worried that the smugglers might have seen us racing away from the house earlier, and when they raced by us on Joffrey Street, I was sure they were going to stop. When I stepped out in the sunlight again, I noticed that I couldn't see Sarah. I started to call her name, but two men that I recognized as Charlie and Sam, the smugglers from Saxe Point Park, rushed me from the side of the deck. I could hear Rasputin barking from inside the house.

"Come here, you little brat!" Charlie yelled, as they both raced toward me.

"We're not going to hurt you, kid. We just want to talk to you." he smiled at me with a wicked grin. I turned and headed back toward the house and just managed to open the door and push Rasputin in. I closed and locked it before they could grab me.

"I've called the police, and they're on their way!" I shouted through the door with Rasputin challenging them with his frantic barking.

“You say anything, and your sister is dead!” one of them answered and then it went quiet. I stood there for a moment, thinking, *what am I going to do?* Then I went upstairs with Rassy bounding close behind me, still barking with excitement. I looked out the back kitchen window, and I could see the black van behind our house on Wychbury. I saw the two men get into the front of it and drive away. I stood there with my mouth open. What could I do? They had my sister. If the cops try and get them, they might kill her before they get there. I decided to phone Rickyy. I had to dial the number two times as my mind was reeling with confusion.

“Hi, Ricky, they got Sarah!” I screamed. “I don’t know what to do!”

“Oh, my God!” Ricky said. “We’ve got to tell my dad!”

“No, Ricky. They said they’d kill her if I told the cops!” I argued.

“Well, what are you going to tell your mom and dad tonight?” he countered.

“Good question!” I answered in frustration. “Phone your dad, and we’ll talk to the cops. They’ll know what to do.” I groaned and hung up the phone.

- CHAPTER FOUR -

The Van

It was 4:30 p.m. when the police car rolled up to our house. My mom's car arrived seconds later, and I could hear her footsteps on the stairs as the police followed her into the basement. Ricky was with his dad and another policeman, a lady cop that I didn't recognize, although I had seen her with Ricky's dad before. Mom patted Rassy, who was starting to bark at the policemen and told him to be quiet. He whined but stopped barking and just sniffed at them, finally settling on following everybody upstairs.

"Oh, Billy, what happened to Sarah!" my mom cried at me as she hugged me to her. Tears began to fill my eyes as I stammered that I didn't know; that the smugglers had taken her.

"Why didn't you tell me about this before?" she questioned, as she held me by the shoulders.

"I don't know. I thought you wouldn't listen to us. You're always telling us that we imagine things, so I figured you wouldn't want to know what we thought…" I trailed off in between sniffling and tears.

"Oh, honey, I'm so sorry." she sobbed at me. "You can always tell me anything…from now on, okay?" I was too choked to answer, and the silence was broken by Ricky's dad.

"Billy, Ricky said that they sped away in a black van. Do you know the license plate?" he asked.

"It was on Sarah's notepad, but she has that with her," I replied.

"Think hard, son; maybe you can remember some of it," he encouraged. My mom suggested we go into the living room and sit down. The two police detectives followed us, and Mom motioned for them to sit down. Ricky's dad sat on the sofa, and the lady cop sat in one of the armchairs beside it. Rasputin lied down between me and the police detectives, still wary of these strangers. After about a minute, the lady cop leaned forward and spoke up.

"Billy, I'm Cpl. Evans. Can you remember what the men looked like who took your sister?" she asked as she looked over at me and smiled. She had blonde hair and piercing blue eyes. She reached into her belt pouch and pulled out her notepad and pencil.

"Um, I think the two guys' names were Charlie and Sam," I stammered. "Charlie was the shorter one with light hair and a red beard, and Sam was taller with black hair and a moustache."

As Cpl. Evans wrote frantically. She asked me about how tall they were. I told her that Charlie was about 5' 8'' and Sam was about 6' tall. As she was writing, I remembered the other two.

"There were two others too," I added; "Another guy who seemed to be the leader named Ted and his girlfriend, Cheryl. Ted was also about 6' tall; he wore a black cape and smoked a pipe. He wore a captain's hat."

"And what about his girlfriend?" asked Cpl. Evans.

"Uh, she was short, about 5'2'' and had blonde hair, I think," I replied, looking at Ricky.

"I think her hair was a reddish color with blonde streaks," Ricky added. "I remember because my older sister, Diane, has hers like that." With that, Ricky's dad looked over at his son and then asked me some more questions.

"Billy, do you remember which way the van headed?" he asked.

"They headed back down Wychbury toward Kinver," I answered.

"And can you boys show us where this house is?" he continued.

"Oh, yeah, we sure can!" we both echoed at once. With that, Ricky's dad turned to my mom and told her that he would like to take us to the house to get a better description of it and investigate further.

"But it's not safe!" complained my mom, who stood up out of the chair she was in and hugged me.

"Don't worry, Mrs. Maclean, we won't let anything happen to him," Cpl. Evans reassured her.

"We need the boys with us because they may remember something about the case which will help us find your daughter," broke in Ricky's dad, Sgt. Stevens.

"Okay," Mom said quietly, "but let me know as soon as you find out something." She began to sob again as she hugged me even tighter.

"I'll be okay, Mom. Don't worry." I tried to console her. I really wanted to do something to help get my sister back. She may be a pain sometimes, but I was really worried about her. As we left the house, I could see my mom looking out the front window with Rassy beside her. Also, I knew my father would be home any minute as the police had phoned him too, and I didn't want to be here when he arrived. I didn't know how he would react. He might blame me because I got Sarah into this mess in the first place. I was the older brother, and I should have known better and steered clear of these guys and told them and called the police. I knew what my father would say. He was predictable. I just wanted to do something to solve this case and get Sarah back.

In the squad car, I asked if we could have the back windows open as it was getting very warm after the hot day. Cpl. Evans pushed a button in front of her, and the windows opened. The air was warm, but it was a relief from the heat we felt. Along Lampson Street, Ricky and I saw a few of our friends walking toward Flemings Beach, and we were happy that this police car was unmarked. We didn't need all of their questions any time soon. We sped past, and they didn't notice us.

"I wonder if they're still at the old house," Ricky said quietly.

"I don't know, but I hope there is no trouble. I'm worried about Sarah." I whispered.

"Me too," Ricky said sadly.

When we turned onto Wollaston, Ricky's dad asked us where the house was exactly. Ricky told him it was the last one on the left, just before Dunsmuir Avenue. As the house came into view, my heart began to beat faster, and I felt myself sweat more than the heat was causing. I wondered if they were at the house. I couldn't see the black van anywhere.

"You two stay here in the car while we investigate," ordered Cpl. Evans, as she and Sgt. Stevens prepared to leave the car. We could hear the car police radio crackle as Cpl. Evans explained that we were "...At the perp's hideout, leaving the vehicle to investigate..."

"...10-4 car 7...backup on the way..."

"...10-4 over and out..."said Cpl. Evans and they left the car. Ricky and I looked at each other, not feeling very safe outside in the car, while the two detectives entered the front lawn of the house. We could see Ricky's dad knock on the front door. After knocking several times and not getting any response, they forced the old door jamb and entered the house. It was quiet, and we wondered what they would find. After about 10 minutes, the two detectives came out of the house just as another police car, this time a marked one, came up to the curb from Dunsmuir end of Wollaston. The two detectives started talking to the two beat cops and then came over to us. Sgt. Stevens leaned against the open window and talked to us.

"Okay, boys, we want you to follow us into the house. There is nobody there, and it seems deserted. We need you to tell us what you saw before. You said you were here this afternoon, right?" he questioned us.

"Yes, we were in the basement." I began to explain.

"How did you get into the basement?" he asked.

"Ah, the back door was not secure and well...my sister was able to crawl under it and..." I stammered, feeling guilty about our unlawful entry.

"I see." He cut me off. "Well, just come and let us know what you remember."

With that, we all headed toward the house. The two beat cops were instructed to stay outside just in case the smugglers returned. They were careful to drive their marked car over onto Dunsmuir and walk back to sit in the unmarked car so as not to attract suspicion. After all, these kidnappers had Sarah. We entered the house, and I was surprised at how vacant it looked; not even a couch or chair in the living room. The old hardwood floors seemed treacherous as they creaked underfoot, and there was a lot of dust on them. No maid here. The windows had a yellowish tint which partially blocked out the sun, well that and the heavy, dark drapes over the windows. It looked like the setting for "Tales from the Crypt," which I liked to watch when my mom allowed me to. She was always afraid I would get nightmares from those shows.

In the kitchen, there was an old set of chrome chairs and a table. An old fridge, gold in color, sat derelict with its door open and nothing in it except a bottle of beer, as if someone had left in such a hurry that they hadn't even bothered to close the fridge. Cpl. Evans removed the bottle with a gloved hand and put it into a bag she pulled from a box she carried. She had a bunch of forensic-like stuff in it, powders, tools, chemical sprays, etc. She told us not to touch anything as she put the bottle into an evidence bag and left it on the table. There were no drapes on the windows in the kitchen, and I could see into the backyard, which was full of trees and bushes right up to the windows. Then as I was looking around, I could hear Ricky's dad calling Cpl. Evans from the hallway. She went in his direction, and we slowly followed. There was a door at the back of the hallway which led into the basement, and that was where Sgt. Stevens was calling from. We proceeded down the stairs and saw him standing in front of the tool bench that we had seen when we were hiding in the basement before. On the bench, there were various old tools, but he was pointing at something else. It was shiny and round with buttons on it.

As we got a closer look, I could see that it had a small, blinking red light flashing from the center of it.

"It probably came out of the trunk." Ricky reasoned.

"What trunk?" asked his dad.

"Remember, Dad? The one I told you about when we were here before." Ricky explained.

"Yes. The one with the padlock and the helmet-like thing inside it?" continued his father. "Hmm! Bag it but be careful with it. We don't know what it does!" he glanced at Cpl. Evans. She proceeded to pick it up gingerly and put it into another evidence bag which she immediately took upstairs to her box of tools.

"Anything else you remember?" Detective Stevens said as he began to survey the basement.

"We hid behind those boxes." I offered, pointing behind us. The detective carefully moved over behind the boxes and came back with a piece of rope in his hands.

"Hmm, maybe used to tie someone up with?" he asked himself more than either of us. Then as the corporal returned, he handed the rope to her and told her to bag it as it might have fingerprints on it. Had Sarah been tied up there? I think the detective was thinking the same thing.

"Well, it looks like they've abandoned the house, so we'll leave and get those patrolmen outside to do a little quiet surveillance while we wait for the forensic evidence." Ricky's dad said as he headed up the basement stairs. We followed slowly. I wonder where my sister could be.

"Maybe we should investigate Saxe Point Park. There might be something you two have overlooked," said Cpl. Evans.

"Or something you might remember," finished Detective Stevens.

When we were outside, I noticed that the wind had picked up and it was blowing in some dark clouds. It looked like rain.

"Billy, what is your phone number again?" Ricky's dad called to me as he leaned against his car that the patrolmen were vacating. He had his cell phone in his hand. Cpl. Evans was talking to the two officers beside the car.

"You two stay here for a while, just in case they come back to the house. Call us immediately if you see anything suspicious or if they return."

"Yes, Corporal," they both responded mechanically. Sgt. Stevens turned to me.

"That phone number, son?"

"Ah…382-5965", I responded. It took me a second because I usually don't phone my own number. I wondered how my mom was doing and thought about how my father would react as the detective punched in the number.

"Hello, Mrs. MacLean?" he started. "Yes, he's alright…No, there wasn't any sign of them or Sarah at the house." He continued… "We'd like to take the boys to Saxe Point Park to investigate further…Okay then, I'll phone you when we are on our way back….Don't worry…Goodbye."

And with that, he ended the conversation and returned his phone to its case in his belt. Cpl. Evans moved away from the two patrolmen and told us to get into the unmarked police car. Ricky and I got in the back seat as the two detectives slid into the front, and Sgt. Stevens started the engine. I took one last look at the strange old house. The wind was whipping the bushes and trees around the side of the house, leaves were flying, and the doors and windows rattled. It reminded me of Dorothy's house in "The Wizard of Oz." I expected it to lift off of its foundation at any minute and spiral up toward Munchkin Land. In another minute, we were rolling along down Lampson Street, but as we neared Greenwood Avenue, I spotted a black van coming toward us. I strained to see the license plate as I dug my elbow into Ricky's ribs and pointed at it.

"Look, Ricky!" I said in a hoarse whisper. "That looks like the black van!"

"Yeah, you're right!" he answered. "Dad, that black van looks like the one we told you about!"

"Are you sure?" questioned his dad and Cpl. Evans took out her notepad and pencil. The wind was gusting harder now, and the rain was starting to fall. As we approached the van, it was more difficult to see. The rain was like a cloudburst, and it began to rattle on the windows and cause sheets of water to stream down. We couldn't quite make out the numbers of the license, but I was pretty sure I saw TAN. I couldn't make out the rest of it. When the van passed us close to Bewdley Avenue, Sgt. Stevens turned left and did a quick U-turn near Ann Hathaway's Cottage, and headed back up Lampson Street. The rain was slowing, and we could just see the car turning right down Kinver Street toward the Marina. We sped up to close the gap, but when we turned onto Kinver, the van was nowhere in sight.

"This is car 16 to 24 over." Cpl. Evans spoke over the radio.

"Car 24 over," came the response.

"Any sighting of a black van, license Tom Adam Nancy 2 5 6, over," she continued.

"No, quiet here 16, over."

"24, join our pursuit. Go south on Dunsmuir…Rendezvous at the marina. Over." Cpl. Evans directed.

"Roger, on our way. Car 24 over and out." The other patrolman answered.

Ricky and I looked at each other. We were part of a pursuit! This was getting exciting, although I was getting a little worried about my sister. What if the culprits spotted us? They had said no cops or else! When we saw the marina, I noticed a boat that looked a lot like the one we had seen at Saxe Point Park pulling out of the marina. We were too late! They were getting away! The detectives noticed it, too, and stepped from the car to get a closer look. Sgt. Stevens warned us to stay in the car, or we might attract suspicion, especially if one of the smugglers was still around the dock. That's when we noticed the black van speed away from the parking lot west onto Kinver. Just after it disappeared, car 24 came down Head Street to the marina and parked across the street just out of sight of the dock.

"Hold your position 24" Cpl. Evans dictated from the ghost car.

"Tell them to follow the van!" Sgt. Stevens called back to his partner as he was halfway across the street to the marina.

"24, head down Kinver in pursuit of the black van. He might be headed for Saxe Point Park." She yelled across the police phone.

"Keep your distance. No siren! I repeat, No siren!"

"On our way, over," responded the patrolmen, and they sped off down Kinver.

"Car 24, 16, this is car 12. We have just spotted your black van on Lampson, south of Kinver, headed to the ocean…are in pursuit, over". Another patrol car had joined the chase.

"Car 12, stay well back. No siren, and do not intercept.... I repeat....Do not intercept!" Cpl. Evans barked over the police phone.

"Roger that 16, Car 12 over and out," came the reply. I was really concerned about my sister now. Surely, the smugglers would know that the cops were following them! Sgt. Stevens entered the car and radioed dispatch.

"This is car 16. Request a run on a black van, license Tom Adam Nancy...2.5.6. Also, advise Coast Guard.... Be on the lookout for a 25-foot yellow cabin cruiser, white top...dual flags...headed south out of West Bay Marina...May be registered with harbor authorities on either side...over." he directed over the radio.

"16, this is dispatch. Have your information...will advise...over." the reply came back. This was really getting interesting. I looked over at Ricky, and we both were wondering what was going to happen next, as the car pulled away from the curb, and we followed the pursuit. We were barely onto Lampson Street when a dispatch came over the radio.

"This is car 12...Sergeant, you're not going to believe us..." We could hear the lead pursuit car.

"This is 16. Repeat, car 12, over." The detective responded excitedly.

"It disappeared...It just was there...and then...nothing!" came the estranged call.

"What do you mean, disappeared? ...Over".

"It was right in front of us...and then it was gone... Into thin air! ...Over".

"Stay put, 12. We are on our way, over and out." Sgt. Stevens put the radio handpiece down and looked over to his partner, who turned and looked at us in the back seat.

"Did he say it vanished, Dad?" Ricky asked his father, his eyes like saucers. "You heard it, Son," answered his dad shaking his head. "This is starting to sound like something out of the X-Files!" Nobody said any more as we sped toward Saxe Point Park.

- CHAPTER FIVE –

Somewhere Else

Sarah felt a jolt accompanied by a sense of motion sickness as the road, wind, rain, and trees disappeared in a blur as if they had entered a swimming pool. It was like when you dove into the deep end, and everything was distorted; sound, light, vision. The difference was that it seemed as if they were being sucked into a tunnel whose sides were a hazy mass of color, light and sound.

Then, after what seemed like a few seconds, there was another jolt, and they stopped moving as if they were in a jet and came to a harsh emergency landing, but without the squealing of brakes. That's when she closed her eyes, expecting a crash. The van lurched forward and then stopped. The engine had died. Sarah carefully opened her eyes. Her stomach churned, and she felt sick; her head was spinning. Images whirled in front of her terrified eyes. Where were they? What was she seeing? Then she passed out……. When she came to, she was in a basement room. She could faintly see walls with no windows, but there was an open door, and light was spilling in from another room. She could hear voices. She tried to get up, but she couldn't move her arms or legs. She was tied to the bed she lay in. She struggled, but it was no use, so she listened and took in her surroundings as best she could.

"Charlie, have you lined up the coordinates yet?" She recognized the voice. It was the leader, Ted.

"Just about there," Charlie answered.

"When did he say we could get this transferred?" That was his girlfriend, Cheryl, she remembered.

"Tomorrow afternoon," Ted answered. Then the conversations ceased. Sarah was trying to see how she was strapped down when she noticed someone at the door. She quickly pretended to be asleep and squinted through partially closed eyes to see who it was. She recognized Cheryl come in, lean over her and check to see if she was still asleep, so Sarah closed her eyes and relied on her ears to tell her when she left. After a minute or so, she heard footsteps going away from the bed and slowly opened her eyes to see Cheryl exit the room. She wished that she had Rickyy's spy tools right now. He would have a hidden knife or something to cut these ropes with. She strained to get her arm loose from the loop around her wrist, but it was too tight. She would have to just listen and keep trying to get herself free. As she strained to loosen the ropes at her wrists, they relaxed a little. Maybe she could undo it enough to slip her arm free if she kept trying. She had never been known as a quitter. As she tugged, she listened for more conversation from the other room.

"No, she's still sleeping," Cheryl said. Obviously, answering if Sarah was awake yet.

"Probably, better that way; less trouble." She heard one of the men say. Then they were quiet, and all Sarah could do was struggle and listen and wish she had Laura Croft's skills like in the movie Tomb Raider……

*_*_*_*_*

When the detectives and the boys reached Saxe Point Park, they could see the puzzled patrolmen from both vehicles standing, looking along the roadway into the park as if trying to pick up clues about the whereabouts of the missing van. The two detectives and the boys exited the vehicle and walked over to the patrolmen.

"Tell me exactly what you saw," demanded Sgt. Stevens, while Cpl. Evans had pulled out her notepad, ready to take down their statement.

"It's like we said over the radio, Sarg, the van just disappeared. It was in front of us about half a block, and it suddenly went wavy…blurry… like something passing through a force field or something. You know, like on Star Trek. Then it disappeared in a flash like it entered a doorway. We saw a rippling affect in the air, and it disappeared. We just about cracked up when I put on the brakes because it was so sudden, and we couldn't take our eyes off of it," said the taller officer who had corporal stripes on his sleeve.

"How do we write up this report?" asked the other, more junior officer, obviously very agitated.

"You don't!" ordered Ricky's dad. "You leave out the disappearing part and just say that you lost the suspect vehicle as you neared Saxe Point Park. Is that clear?"

"Yes, sir, but I know what I saw!" argued the younger officer.

"I do not doubt what you saw," countered Sgt. Stevens, "I'm just saying that we don't need to bring a bunch of questioning upper-level brass into this. Better for everyone if it stays quiet for now, right?"

"Yes, sir," all of the officers, including the two from car 24, replied.

"Were there any civilian witnesses?" Cpl. Evans asked.

"Not that we noticed," answered the corporal, hesitantly.

"You think that we should ask around the neighborhood?"

"Yes, but be very vague about what you are saying to them. Stick with the black van and how you lost it when you were pursuing it. If they saw anything else, let them tell you, not the other way around!" directed Detective Stevens. With that, the other officers began to head toward the houses close to the park.

The detectives turned to us as we began to head back to the car, and Cpl. Evans suggested that we be driven back to my place, as they wanted to talk with our parents. Ricky's mom was going to go over to my house anyway because they wanted both of us boys to be together while they figured out what to do. As we headed toward my house, I noticed that something had fallen out of the evidence box that had been briefly in the car, when Cpl. Evans was putting the items from the house into it. I carefully reached down under the passenger seat and lifted up the bag. It had the circular object in it from the basement of the house. I slipped it quickly into my pocket. As I did so, Sgt. Stevens caught my eye in his rear-view mirror.

"You okay back there, Billy?" he asked.

"Uh…yes, sir." I stammered. "Just my shoelace…untied," I lied. Ricky looked over at me, knowing that was not the truth, but not saying anything as his dad spoke again.

"Okay, then. Now listen, you two! I don't want you upsetting your parents, so do not say anything about what those patrolmen said they saw. Is that clear?" He commanded as we came to a stop outside of my house.

"Yes, sir!" we both echoed at the same time, looking at each other with wide eyes, our hearts pounding. As we got out of the car, I could see my mom, dad, and Ricky's mom coming out of the basement door to join us. Both of our moms hugged us as if we had been the ones kidnapped, and I could tell that my mom had been crying. I still felt bad about Sarah and wondered what my father was going to say as I peeked around my mom's shoulder to see his stern expression.

"Well, what have you found out? Where is my daughter?" he demanded even before the detectives could enter the house.

"Why don't we get out of the street first, Mr. Maclean?" suggested Sgt. Stevens as he started to walk toward the basement door.

"Humph!" my father answered, turned and headed toward the house. Once inside, in the living room with Rassy bounding about at our feet, the detective suggested that we boys go to my room as the adults talked about what had happened. Ricky and I gladly took Rasputin and went to my bedroom. When I had closed the door, Ricky burst out in a harsh whisper, "What do you have in your pocket?"

"You remember when we saw that round object with the shining button on it at the house?" I answered excitedly.

"Yeah!" Ricky looked at my pocket with his saucer eyes as I slowly pulled the bag out with the round shiny object inside. Rassy whined at it and tried to sniff at it.

"No, boy!" I discouraged him and held it up from his muzzle. He backed away reluctantly and whined again as he settled down on his haunches with his eyes fixed on the shining object.

"Wow!" Ricky said as he reached out to the bag. "Let me see it!"

"Be careful, Ricky!" I cautioned as I handed it to him.

"I wonder what it does?" he queried with his best James Bond imitation.

"Don't touch anything! Especially that button on it. I have a feeling that has something to do with the helmet thing." I said worriedly.

"Don't worry! I just want to look at it." Ricky assured me. "Did you notice these strange markings on it before?" he continued, running his finger along the etched symbols on the curved surface of the small object.

"No! What do they look like? Let me see!" I demanded as I reached for the object. The figures looked like some ancient form of Egyptian or Sumerian writing with little wedges, but they also included spirals and curved lines. I remembered the symbols when we studied ancient Egypt and Mesopotamia in Social Studies last year, and I don't remember any that looked quite like these.

"Let's copy the symbols. Maybe Professor Adams at the University can help us identify them." I suggested.

"Okay. Have you got some paper and a pencil?" Ricky asked.

"Yeah, over on my desk." With that, I took the object, which still blinked mysteriously at us, and placed it carefully on the desk top. Rassy got up, stretched lazily, whined and followed us to the desk wagging his tail as if he agreed with our efforts. I handed Ricky a pencil and paper, and we both attempted to duplicate the strange symbols:

When we finished, we both agreed that Ricky was more of an artist and decided to take his picture to the professor. I carefully put my piece of paper inside an envelope from my desk, and hid it inside my copy of Harry Potter and the Philosopher's Stone. Just as I did that, there was a knock at the door. I quickly put the object inside my desk drawer and got up to answer it. My mom was at the door telling us that it was time for Ricky to go home with his mom now so, we both left my room with Rasputin at our heels and headed for the basement. The detectives had already left and Ricky's mom was waiting in the driveway with my dad. They were discussing the latest events with worried looks on their faces.

"Come on, Ricky. We've got to get home and have some dinner. It's getting late," she directed.

"Call you tomorrow," Ricky said as he caught up with his mom at her car.

"Yeah, see you then," I answered. As they left up the street, I turned to look at my dad, still wondering about his reaction to all of this and still feeling guilty about my sister.

"I'm sorry about Sarah, Dad!" I offered sadly. To my surprise and relief, he didn't scold me but rather, spoke quietly.

"I know, son. It wasn't your fault. These smugglers are dangerous and you have to keep clear of them. Let the police handle it. They know what they're doing." His voice was soft and halting. I had never heard him sound so sad before, except for the time when grandpa passed away last winter. I'm sure he was fighting back tears as he gave me a hug, and I started to feel tears well up in my eyes. All of the emotions of the day's events started to flow out of me as I whimpered in his arms.

"It's okay. It'll all work out. Sarah will be alright. You'll see." He reassured me, and I felt closer to my dad than I had in a long time. We slowly went back into the house where mom was making dinner. She looked up with a very unhappy expression, as if all of the hope in her was gone, and she trudged around the kitchen getting dinner ready like a zombie. I'd never seen my mom like this before. It was scary. I think I liked it better when they were mad at me. Now I felt like I had been dropped into The Twilight Zone. All through dinner, no one spoke. I think we were all stunned. Then the phone rang. I thought we were all going to jump through the roof. My heart started racing again as I imagined the kidnappers calling for a ransom. But they were going to make millions on their stolen merchandise. They didn't need kidnap money. I could hear my mom on the phone.

"...Yes, well, at least you know where they might be................Is there anything that we can do to help?......Okay, we'll wait for your call....Thank you, Detective." I heard her put the receiver down and shuffle back to the kitchen.

"Well? What did he say?" my father asked in a monotone.

"Nothing new really; they have traced a signal that the United States Air Force said is sent out by a device that was stolen from the Smithsonian Institute last month. Detective Stevens said that the signal registered somewhere in Asia! I think he said southern Russia! Do you think Sarah is somewhere in Russia!?" Mom asked, open-mouthed with shock.

"Russia! How the Hell would they get to Russia so quickly?" my father growled angrily. I knew he must be really upset because he never swears. Then I started thinking about how the van had disappeared. Maybe it was like on Star Trek. Maybe they dematerialized and then rematerialized somewhere else. Cool, I thought. With my head filled with imaginary places...other worlds...other where's...other when's...I asked if I could leave the table and get ready for bed. My parents both looked at me strangely, because usually they have to tell me to get ready for bed. My mom nodded and I left them to their confusion. In my bedroom, I took out the round shiny device in my desk and stared at it. Its red flashing light was hypnotic.

I started to dream about where Sarah might be...I could see people wearing Russian clothes and talking in Russian in a building with spires on the top and barbed wire fencing all around. I was agent Bond, James Bond, looking for the Russians who stole the Interstellar Regenerator from the Americans. I had followed a secret homing beacon concealed in the device. The Russian guards were crossing back and forth in front of the gate to the structure. I couldn't enter that way. Ah-hah! I spotted a trellis leading over the windows up to the second story, which had a balcony. I just had to sneak past the guards and climb the trellis...

As I dreamed, suddenly, the round flashing device in my hand began to hum. It startled me and I put it down on my desk. My hands began to shake as my heart started racing again. I was scared. As I watched, the surface of the strange circular object transformed into a glass-like prism. Shapes began to appear like looking through a small porthole. I could see a room. Then the face of one of the smugglers walked by in front of it. It was the one called Charlie. I knew because of his red beard. Next, the image changed to a wall with a table. Ted was sitting at it with Cheryl. On the table was the helmet. Its buttons were lit up and there was a humming sound. The trunk lay beside the table. Ted was talking on a transmitter, like a short- wave radio set.

"Roger A-1. We will have delivery of the package at 0900-03-08-28 over.... We copy that....at E30...N60...over.........All clear at this end, over.......One problem to note......The D-105 is missing.......No, it was not in the package, over......Yes, the rest of the delivery will be made at rendezvous stated, over and out." He put down the speaker phone and turned to Cheryl.

"Is she awake yet? We will need to get moving in the morning." He spoke firmly to her.

"I think she is waking up. We should feed her before tomorrow. She has been sick because of the drugs, and we don't need her dying on us!" she said with real concern.

"Well, get some nourishment down her then. We don't need a murder rap added to this. Stealing is one thing; murder is another. Go check her again." He directed.

Cheryl rose from her chair and headed across the room to a doorway that obviously led to another room. That must be where they were keeping Sarah. I wished I could see into that room, but the scan through the prism didn't seem to reach that far. My guess was that it only worked where the helmet was located. That would explain why the room was clear where it sat on the table. As the humming stopped, the images through the prism went wavy, blurry and finally disappeared altogether as the object's shiny metallic finish reappeared. I sat back, stunned. After I had gathered my senses, I reached into my desk and pulled out a pencil and notepad. I quickly began scribbling notes of what I had heard and seen:

Somewhere in Russia...........basement rooms...........Ted...Cheryl......Charlie......helmet.........short wave radio......delivery of package at 0900-03-08-28......at location...E30...N60... .D105...missing....Sarah in other room...sick...

I looked at my notes and thought about how important they were. I've got to talk to Detective Stevens. No, I'll call Rickyy, I thought. I crept into the hallway and removed the portable phone from the receiver, and brought it back to my bedroom. I dialed Ricky's number. I was shaking again as I waited for someone to pick up the receiver...

"Hello?" It was his mom.

"Oh, hi, Mrs. Stevens; could I please speak with Ricky?" I asked eagerly.

"Yes, just a minute, Billy," she said quietly. I could hear her calling Ricky to the phone in the background and then the clunk of the receiver as she put it down. A few seconds later, I heard someone pick it up.

"Hello?"

"Ricky, remember that circular object I have that was in the trunk?" I blurted out nervously.

"Yeah!" he responded.

"Well, it is some kind of seeing device! I could see the smugglers through it. Where they were and what they were doing." I quickly explained; my heart pounding.

"Wow! Where are they?" he whispered sharply.

"Somewhere in Russia, I think," I answered, a little calmer.

"Russia? What should we do?"

"I don't know, Ricky! Could you come over, do you think?" I asked.

"No, mom said I have to get to bed early tonight. After all that has happened, I think she is worried about me. I could come over in the morning, though," he offered.

"Okay. I'm not going to do anything until we talk tomorrow. See you then, Ricky." I said with a little relief in my voice, as I did not want to make this decision on my own. I went back to my room and got ready for bed. When I finally crawled under the covers that night, I felt very uneasy with that thing in my desk. When my mom came in to check on me, I pretended that I was asleep. I wasn't feeling up to any more of her worrisome smothering. My mind was swirling with ideas about what to do tomorrow. Should I talk to Detective Stevens? Should I tell my parents about the object? Should I try and put it together myself with Ricky's help? I finally drifted off to sleep by continuing my James Bond movie in my head.... James reaches the second story of the mansion and enters the room by an upstairs window. He uses his handy magnetic latch opener that Q had perfected for him. As he enters, a guard checking the rooms notices him and charges......

- CHAPTER SIX -

D-105

Morning came with a knock on my bedroom door. My mom entered and shook me. I sleepily looked up at her worried face.

"Billy, you have to get up. There are men here from the FBI and the CIA to talk to you!" she stared wide-eyed as the words stormed out. "Something about a secret device that was stolen from the Smithsonian Institute. They say you have information for them about it. What's going on? Are you in some kind of trouble? What does this have to do with Sarah's kidnapping?"

"Mom, those smugglers took a secret object from the Smithsonian, and they are going to sell it to somebody for millions of dollars and Sarah, Ricky and I saw it, and then they kidnapped Sarah and she's been taken to Russia or somewhere…"

I tried to tell her everything, but I was cut off by my father yelling that I'd better hurry up as the agents needed to talk to me right away.

"Okay." My mom said finally. "Just get dressed and come out." With that, she hugged and kissed me and left the room. I was shaking, my heart pounding, as I pulled off my pajamas and put on shorts and a T-shirt. I slowly turned the knob to the door and crept out into the hall. Just then, the doorbell rang. When I reached the living room, I saw four men in black suits. They rose as I entered and introduced themselves. My dad and mom sat on the two chairs. The first one extended his hand to me.

"Hi, Billy, I'm Captain Moore, and this is Sergeant Davis. We're from the CIA."

"And we're Agents Dobbs and Scarlet of the FBI." The third man said as he rose, and his partner, a lady, stood beside him. The men all had short hair and were clean-shaven; all were over six feet. The two from the CIA had a very military posture and stern appearance. The two from the FBI seemed more relaxed. The woman looked very pretty with auburn hair and green eyes. Her dainty figure contrasted with her businesslike demeanor.

"We hear you've had quite a summer already!" she said, raising her eyebrows.

Before I could answer, Ricky came in from the kitchen, closely followed by Detective Stevens and Corporal Evans. I nodded to Ricky, and he came over to stand beside me.

"We want you two to start from the beginning." One of the CIA gentlemen began. He was older than the others and seemed to be in charge. His salt and pepper hair made me guess he was around fifty or so. Everyone sat back down, and Ricky and I told them all about our adventure so far. When we started talking about the trunk and its contents, they stopped us and questioned us some more about what we saw in it. They looked puzzled when we only talked about the helmet and not the round circular object, but didn't seem willing to tell us about what we had left out. I heard one of them mumble D-105 several times to his partner. At that point, Rasputin came bounding into the living room, and my father told me to take him to the basement. I asked if he could stay, and my dad relented, making him sit down by the door to the kitchen, which he did despite our company, although I noticed that his ears were pricked up and his eyes followed the visitors' every move. After our debriefing, I asked if Ricky and I could go out and play. My dad said that would be okay, but we had to take Rasputin with us because he needed a walk, as he had been cooped up in the house for four days. I reluctantly agreed and headed for my room with Ricky and Rasputin close behind. When we got to my room, I closed the door and discussed our next step with Ricky.

"We've got to find out what those symbols mean," I said excitedly.

"Yeah, but Billy, maybe we should have told the detectives about the object," Ricky suggested uncertainly.

"Not yet. I want to put this whole thing together first. I want to find out what's going on. If we just give it to them, they won't tell us what they know or find out." I countered. So, we headed outside with the object safe in my pocket and Rasputin on a leash. We took him around the block and down to Saxe Point Park. There were police still there from the other day, looking at the paths, and they were down in the cove. Ricky and I walked Rassy toward the cove and peered down to see what they were doing. They had some sophisticated equipment down there, and I could see some of the FBI agents or CIA types mulling about talking and looking carefully at various objects on the beach. We crept closer to the edge to see and pulled Rasputin down with us, which brought a soft whine from him, but he soon quieted down. We could see a machine with an antenna-like device on the top and a man speaking into it

"....2 degrees south by southwest...15 degrees north by northeast...." It sounded like some sort of telemetry. Were they trying to locate something? There were a few boats along the seashore, and suddenly one of the men on the boat nearest us called to the two FBI agents to come aboard, as they had spotted a suspicious craft out in the strait. The two agents hopped on board the vessel, which quickly headed out of the cove toward the American side. Meanwhile, the men combing the cove continued to hunt for something along the beach.

"It was here!" One of them said. "Traces are evident among the pebbles, and we found some along that pathway." He pointed in our direction as he said that, and we quickly lowered our heads from view.

"Let's sweep a few more times. It might be here somewhere, and if we find it, we can track the smugglers." The speaker was a tallish, graying gentleman who appeared to be in charge of the investigation.

We decided to head back to the house before we were discovered, so we quietly crept back up the path and headed home. "I wonder what they were looking for." Ricky voiced what we were both thinking.

"I don't know, but I wonder if it was the "D-105"?" I said, patting my pocket.

"Let's get back so we can go to the University of Victoria," I continued. "I want to show those symbols to Professor Reynolds. He's a Linguist and an authority on ancient cultures as well as being interested in extraterrestrials. I know him because he is a friend of my dad's. I met him last summer when dad was taking some language courses, and they talked about UFOs. Dad has a scrapbook full of newspaper articles and the Project Bluebook Report. There is some really neat stuff in there."

"My dad says that's a bunch of baloney," Ricky said.

"Yeah, well, a lot of people don't think so, Ricky," I stated.

"I know. I'm not sure what to believe after what we've seen lately!" he agreed. When we got home and dropped Rassy off, I asked my mom if we could get a ride to the University as her way to work took her near there, because she picked up her friend, Alison, who also worked downtown. She said she would drop us off after I had to explain to her that we wanted to look at some neat displays in the University Centre. There was a display of ancient Native cultural objects currently showing, and Mom was all for me doing something educational. We rode silently in the car until we were going north along Shelbourne Street when an ambulance came screaming from behind us. We carefully pulled over with all the other vehicles and watched the ambulance zoom by, siren blaring toward Gordon Head. Mom said there was often an accident out on the Pat Bay Highway, and the emergency vehicles used Shelbourne as part of their route to get to Royal Jubilee Hospital. After the ambulance passed, we continued up Shelbourne. At Mackenzie Avenue, we turned right and headed to the University of Victoria. When we reached Ring Road, I was surprised at all of the traffic in the summer time. Mom explained that a lot of people took summer courses at UVic., and she was contemplating upgrading her Accounting at the university next year. She dropped us off right in front of the University Centre and told us to take the bus home. We had summer bus passes, so it was free. Mom said it was a good idea because we never would be stranded that way, and Ricky had a pass as well. She also said that she expected us to both be back by dinner time, and we closed the car doors and waved goodbye as she drove away along Ring Road.

"We'd better head toward the displays and take in some of them so when our moms question us, we will know what to say," Ricky suggested.

"Good idea, Ricky!" I agreed, and we headed into the University Centre. It was fairly crowded, and a lady dressed in a traditional costume of the First Nations was handing out pamphlets.

"Welcome!" she said with a beautiful smile.

"Thank you!" we both answered and accepted a pamphlet each. As we glanced through the pages of the small booklet, we noticed the beautiful artwork, sculptured totems and masks along the back walls of the center's foyer.

"Wow! Look at those masks!" Ricky pointed in front of us.

"Yeah! Those are fantastic! Remember the native animal masks we made in school last year? Don't you wish they had turned out like that?" We spent some time looking at the displays, and before we knew it, the afternoon was quickly ending. I glanced at my Harry Potter watch and noticed that it was already 3:15 p.m.

"Ricky, we'd better get going over to Professor Reynold's office before we have to start for home!" I said as I grabbed his arm.

"What time is it?" he asked.

"It's already 3:15!" I answered in earnest. With that, we headed out of the Centre and over to the Social Sciences building, which housed the professor's office. Just as we were nearing the building, I recognized him coming out of the east doorway, headed toward the Library.

"Professor Reynolds!" I called, and he stopped and turned slightly to see who was calling. He didn't recognize me, so as we got close, I called again. He was a medium-built man with a grey beard, small, square glasses and piercing blue eyes. He caught my gaze and strained to see who had addressed him.

"Professor, its Billy Maclean; remember last summer? You and my dad talked about UFOs and stuff?" I said, hoping he would remember.

He looked puzzled for a second and then put his hand forward and said, "Ah, yes! You seemed very interested in the subject, too, if I remember correctly."

"I still am!" I confirmed, shaking his hand. "This is my friend, Ricky Stevens. We've got something very interesting to show you!"

"Pleased to meet you." the professor said as he shook Ricky's hand and then looked over at me. "I'd like to, but I've got an appointment at 3:30, and I'm afraid I'll be late…"

"Professor, you've got to help us!" I broke in. "This is an urgent matter! Please help us!"

He stopped and stared seriously at me. "What is this all about?" he started.

"Help us, and I'll tell you about it," I reassured him as Ricky gave me a doubting look.

"Well, okay then," he said. "Let's go back to my office where my books are, and maybe I can decode whatever you have." He immediately led the way back toward the Social Sciences building. The hallways were busy with student and teacher traffic as they moved to various classes. Everybody seemed preoccupied. I'd often noticed when up here with my father that everybody seemed to have their nose in a book or were deep in intellectual conversation, except that is, for the sun worshippers who played Frisbee and flew kites on the campus lawns. The environment always seemed so peaceful, not like my school playground where kids were yelling and roughhousing at every recess. Sometimes I wished I was older and could attend a college.

At the professor's office, I noticed pictures on the walls of ancient tribal peoples; one of Botswana tribes from Africa, one of an Inuit tribe from northern Canada and one of a Hawaiian canoe race. I wondered if Professor Reynolds had traveled to such exotic places or not.

"Well, let's see what you've got." He suddenly spoke and focused my attention.

"Uh, here you go. You can see interesting shapes like written symbols on the side of this circular object." I said as I pulled the "D-105" from my pocket. The professor reached over and began to look more closely at it as he took it into his hand.

"Oh, my, I don't believe I've ever seen symbols like these!" He said excitedly. "Hum. Look somewhat like Egyptian but too stylized; kind of modern." He mumbled as he ran his fingers over the symbols which seemed to be carved into the object. "Where did you get this?" he questioned with piercing eyes that stared at me intently.

"We found it by the beach," I said in half-truth, not wanting to tell him the real story and doubting if he would believe me anyway.

"Which beach?" He pressed.

"Along the ocean in Esquimalt," I offered, afraid to meet his gaze and feeling a little uncomfortable. Professor Reynolds picked up his magnifying glass and studied the piece under the light at his desk.

"This metal seems extremely hard, polished and too smooth to be from an ancient civilization. And this red light that doesn't stop blinking suggests a modern use. You know, I think I've seen writing like this before, from an object that a friend of mine sent me pictures of. They were from "Area 51" in Nevada. They were supposed to be pictures of writing from some objects that crashed near Roswell, New Mexico, in 1947! I've got them somewhere around here." He mumbled again as he began shuffling around in his file cabinet beside his desk. I looked over at Ricky, and he gazed back at me. We both did not know what to say next.

"Ah-hah! Here they are!" the professor declared as he brought a file folder out of the cabinet's second drawer and placed it on his desk. He opened it up, and a moment later, he was spreading several large 81/2" x11" glossy black and white photos over the top of his desk. We both leaned over and stared in amazement as we saw several bits and pieces of shiny objects with strange writing on them that almost exactly resembled our "D-105" object's inscriptions. I continued to stare open-mouthed at the alien pieces with their alien letters!

"Do you know what the symbols…letters mean?" Ricky blurted out.

"No. At least, I don't think so." He explained. "My colleague in Nevada said that they thought the symbols may have dealt with telemetry, aircraft flying control devices or maybe even star charts or solar directions."

"Wow! Really?" Ricky and I both exclaimed at the same time.

"So, do you think this object belongs in an alien spacecraft?" I asked, my heart in my throat again.

"Maybe." The professor said as he scratched his beard thoughtfully. "I suppose it's possible. Was there any other evidence of a UFO near the beach where you found this?" he pressed.

"No, not really," I said, feeling uncomfortable again.

"What do you mean, not really?" he pushed me further.

"There were some suspicious people around at the time." I tried to select my words carefully so that I was not giving him the whole story, but at the same time, I didn't want to lie either.

"Can I take a picture of this object?" Professor Reynolds asked.

Ricky looked at me with a worried expression. "Well, I guess so," I answered. After all, what could I say? No, because it is a stolen artifact from the Smithsonian that has special powers? The professor quickly reached into his top desk drawer and pulled out a digital camera. He placed the object in the center of his desk, surrounded by the pictures from Roswell, and took several shots from different angles and magnifications.

When he was done, I quickly put the object back into my pocket and thanked him for his help. Then I began to push Ricky out of the office, telling the professor that it was time for us to head for home because if we were late for dinner, Mom would ground us for a week. The professor was trying to get us to stop, but I said again that we really had to leave and, with Ricky in tow, headed down the hallway. Dr. Reynolds was still trying to talk to us but was soon cut off by the heavy traffic in the hallways. We ducked into a vacant classroom to hide.

After a few minutes, students started to enter the room, obviously getting ready for a lesson. We quickly exited the room and headed for the southeast doorway. Luckily, the way was clear. No Professor Reynolds. We started running for the bus stop on Ring Road west of the Social Sciences building. A bus was already there picking up passengers. What luck! We boarded it and sat at the back.

"That was close. I thought he was going to keep the object and phone the authorities or something." Ricky said, out of breath from our brief run.

"Yes. I don't think he wanted us to take it with us. I hope he doesn't phone my dad or the local authorities." I looked at Ricky, my eyes wide with worry.

"Oh, well," Ricky sighed. "At least you'll be home for dinner on time for a change." We both laughed at that, and I reached into my pocket to feel the object and reassure myself that it was still there. We were both tired and sat back to enjoy the ride home.
When we finally got off the bus, it was 5:30 p.m. We headed down Greenwood together as Ricky and his folks were staying for dinner.

At my driveway, I saw my dad looking out of the front window with Detective Stevens. When we reached the stairs, Dad called for us to come into the living room. I told Ricky to go ahead as I called to my folks that I needed to use the bathroom. Rushing down the hall, I went into my bedroom and put the D-105 in my desk and then headed for the washroom. When I entered the living room, my mom and dad were standing by the window. Ricky's parents were standing beside them, and Agents Dobbs and Scarlet, the two FBI agents, were sitting on the sofa. Rasputin bounded forward, away from Ricky's side, as I entered the room, and I patted him on the head. My dad quickly told him to lie down, and he ambled over to the doorway by the kitchen, all the time eyeing the two agents carefully.

"Professor Reynolds called me this afternoon. Any idea what he told me, Billy?" my dad started while grimacing at me. My heart started beating fast again as I looked over to my mom, who was frowning at me.

"Y-you mean a-about the object?" I stammered.

"You'd better tell us the whole story, son." This was Agent Dobbs, who looked at me with his intense stare as his partner took out her pad of paper. I told them everything this time, including the fact that the object in question was in my desk drawer in my room.

At that point, Dobbs stopped me and asked to see it. We all

got up and headed for my room. Rasputin followed us in and bounded up onto my bed beside the desk. Everyone huddled around the desk, and I pulled the drawer open. There the object sat, shiny with its flashing lights. Dobbs reached over and took the object from my hand, carefully examining it as he turned it over between his fingers. The lady agent, Scarlet, asked to look more closely at it, and her partner handed it to her. She looked it over carefully and commented that everything looked much the same. I told them about the humming and how it had turned into a window which you could see through and how I had viewed the smugglers' hideout somewhere in Russia when Agent Scarlet dropped the object, which rolled under my bed. Like a flash, Rasputin dove after it. I had trained him to fetch things for me, so I wasn't too surprised, but the consequent gasp by the visitors showed their concern.

"Rassy!" I immediately shouted and leapt after him, but Agent Dobbs stopped me and said it was dangerous and not to go after it. As he started to reach under the bed for the object, Rasputin growled at him, and he brought his hand back up.

"You'd better let the boy retrieve it," My dad said. "Rasputin won't bite him."

"Okay," agreed Agent Dobbs, "but watch you don't touch any of the buttons on the side." Everyone backed away as I gingerly reached under the bed while coaxing Rassy to drop it. He did, and I brought it out to the desk, but Rasputin bumped me as I was placing it on the desk, and I fell over onto Ricky, who went to steady himself on the desk and placed his hand over the object depressing the red button.

Immediately, everything went fuzzy as Ricky, and I lurched forward and away into cloudy, blurry ether, like being underwater. Sound rushed around our ears, and our stomachs felt like we had had one too many rides on the roller coaster at the PNE in Vancouver. Colors blended together and swirled ahead of us as if we were on some supernatural artist's pallet, blues, reds, yellows, purples and greens. My head started to pound, and I felt sicker as I closed my eyes in horror and thought I was going to die!

- CHAPTER SEVEN -

Russia

Then, just as suddenly as it had started, it stopped. I felt an intense lurch in my body, and my swirling senses settled; my head was still swimming. When I opened my eyes, I couldn't believe it. We were standing in front of a house very similar to the one that I had imagined in my dream. It had spires, tall windows and was surrounded by an iron fence that looked very formidable. I slowly regained my senses and looked over to where Ricky was lying on the grass. I strained to see him as it was dark, almost nightfall here, and he was not moving. My head still ached as I got up dizzily and went over and shook him.

"Ricky, you okay?" I turned him over slowly. His eyes were not open, and his body was limp. I frantically started shaking him and calling at him. Finally, he moved his head groggily and opened his eyes.

"What the Hell was that?" he moaned as he clutched his side where he had banged into something.

"Ricky, you okay?" I asked again, afraid that he was badly hurt.

"I…I think so." He stammered as he sat up. "My head is swimming, and my side aches. Where are we anyway?" he asked in confusion.

"I don't know, but I think maybe we are at the place I saw when I looked through that object last night!" I started and then stopped as I noticed that the object had come with us and was lying over by the roadside. I could see its lights still blinking. I got up and went over to pick it up, but suddenly headlights appeared from around a bend in the road, and I leaped back to the darkness beside the iron fence. The vehicle was a dark van. It sped over the ground and almost ran over the object beside the road. As it approached the gate, it stopped, and the gate slowly began to open automatically. I snuck over, picked up the object then quickly darted back to the blackness of the bushes. There I carefully placed the object into my front pocket.

"If we are quick, we can sneak inside behind that van and get into the courtyard, Ricky!" I explained as he looked over at the van.

"Okay, but wait till they've gone inside a little way." Ricky agreed, trying to shake off his grogginess and focus his eyes. "Did you notice any guards?"

"I think I saw two at the front of the house, but they're distracted by the people coming out of the van. Look, you can see them talking." I pointed past the gate to the front of the house, where two heavily armed men were talking to the occupants of the van. The two guys in the van seemed to be giving the guards directions. They headed for the front door of the tall, three-story building, and one of the guards got into the van and started to drive it around to the back of the house as the other guard headed to the other side of the building.

"Now is our chance, Ricky! Let's go!" I started toward the gate with Ricky close behind. We just made it through the gate before it closed and hid behind some bushes halfway to the front steps.

"Do you think Sarah's in there?" Ricky asked, his breath in short spurts.

"I'd bet on it. This place looks exactly like the one I saw through the prism!" I stated boldly while reaching to feel the D-105 in my pocket. "I wonder if there is another way into it."

"How about around the back where that guard went? There is usually a back door to most places, and they're always less guarded than the front." Ricky reasoned. We headed toward the back of the house. The driveway continued around the stone building through some more bushes and into a backyard with a patio, swimming pool and extensive lawns. We couldn't help but notice the austere magnificence of this castle. It had stone walls with tall spires and large Tudor-style windows with shutters. I think I saw at least five chimneys, three with smoke lazily streaming out of them. There was an extensive walkway all around the top, like a lookout with what appeared to be gun turrets along the sides. It made me think of Hogwarts in the Harry Potter stories. We skulked close to the bushes near the building. We were ready to dive into the foliage at the first sign of guards. Just at the corner of the last high spire, we noticed two guards coming back toward us.

"Quick!" I whispered to Ricky. And I swiftly dove into a big group of laurel bushes near the wall. Ricky followed suit, and we huddled in the cool of the green leaves while trying to hold our breath. As the darkness fell, it helped conceal us even more. The two guards dutifully marched past us without as much as a second look. We waited until they were around the corner before we snuck out of the laurel. From there, we easily made our way to the back of the house, where we could see the guard parking the van inside a huge, six-car garage.

"Hurry, I think we can sneak into the garage before the doors close!" I spoke hoarsely and headed toward the side of the house closest to the far door. Ducking quickly into the garage, I dropped on all fours behind a beautiful Mercedes. Ricky jumped in behind me and landed by the car's rear tire.

"Oof!" he exclaimed.

"Shh!" I cautioned as I slowly raised myself to my knees and peered through the side windows of the Mercedes to see where the guard was. He was just closing the van's side door and heading toward a door at the back of the huge garage. Just before he closed the door behind him, he closed the garage door and turned off the lights. We were in darkness.

"Wow! Some rich guy lives here!" Ricky said as he rubbed his eyes and started to stand up and look around the huge garage.

"No kidding!" I agreed. I, too, stood up and took in our surroundings. There had to be six cars here; the Mercedes, the van, a Corvette, a Cadillac, a Jeep and even a Hummer! It was impressive! There was a complete workshop with all kinds of tools, an area with chairs, a sofa and a TV. We even saw a fridge! Perfect! We were both very thirsty. Quietly and carefully, we headed for the area with the TV and fridge. When we opened the fridge door, we were surprised to see bottles of beer, wine and lots of sodas. I grabbed a Coke, and Ricky went for an Orange Crush, his favorite. We chugged the drinks and sat back on the chair and sofa.

"Well, what do you think we should do now?" Ricky asked as he stretched out on the sofa.

"Let's rest for a bit and then figure out a way of finding Sarah," I whispered in between quick swallows.

"Bu-urp!" Ricky was drinking his pop too quickly.

"Be quiet! They might hear us!" I cautioned.

"Oops! Sorry man, but it was either that or explode!" he giggled.

"Shh!" I tried to be serious, but I laughed as well. Suddenly, I felt a heat in my pocket! It was the D-105 heating up again. I took it out of my pocket and gazed at it.

"Ricky, this thing is going funny again!" I whispered hoarsely.

"Oh, my God!" Ricky was staring at it with his eyes like saucers. I placed the object down on the table beside the sofa and watched as it began to go cloudy and turn into a prism-like window again.

"What's that?" Ricky stared as the "object-window" showed us an image of a room with a bed.

"That looks like a bed, and it looks like Sarah on it with her hands and feet tied!" I whispered, horrified.

"Is she okay?"

"I can't tell, but she looks okay. I think she might be asleep."

"We've got to get her out of there!" Ricky said with genuine concern in his voice. As we looked longer at the image, we saw Cheryl come into the room and talk to Sarah, but there was no response from the form lying on the bed. A moment later, the image changed to another room where there appeared to be a table, chairs and a counter with electronic equipment. It was the same area I had viewed earlier from my bedroom. I could see Ted, the leader of the smugglers talking on a headset. "...Well, okay then, the time is set. Next week at 1300 hours at the rendezvous point... Nobody but your contact, Yuri... Cheryl will be there...Yes, don't worry.... Over and out…" At that point, the image began to fade, and the D-105 quickly went cloudy again.

"Wow, did you see that?" Ricky whispered in awe.

"Yeah, it was just like in my bedroom," I answered, but I was thinking more about Sarah. If they had set up the meeting place, they wouldn't need Sarah after the money is transferred next week. She was not safe! Then, the D-105 began to go hazy and lose its image. Finally, it went back to its original form.

"Let's go!" I said as I put the D-105 back into my pocket. I got up and headed for the door to the inside of the house. Ricky followed close behind. I slowly tried the doorknob, and it opened. Gently, I pushed the door open. The hallway inside was dark. We moved down the corridor, feeling our way along the wall.

"Remember, we're looking for a basement door," I whispered as we came to our first doorway. It was slightly ajar, so I carefully pushed it open a crack and looked inside. It was a bedroom.

"Not this one," I whispered back and stepped toward the next door. Suddenly, lights came on, and we could hear footsteps coming our way.

"Quick!" whispered Ricky as he pulled me back and through the door behind us, "in here!" As I closed the door behind us, I could hear the footsteps closer now. We held our breath and prayed they would not enter this room. Looking around the room, we could see only a small closet to hide in.

"In there!" I pointed to it, and we quickly headed for it. We seemed to be in that closet for hours, but we knew it was only minutes. I thought of looking at the D-105 again, but it had cooled down, and the window would not show, so I left it in my pocket.

"Let's check it out," I said to Ricky, and he slowly opened the closet door, and we both gazed out into a dark bedroom with no sound. I went over to the hall door and put my ear to the wood. Nothing.

"I think it's clear!" I whispered to Ricky. I felt unsure but ready to go on. We both took a deep breath as I slowly opened the hall door. Nobody! Good! We slowly headed up the hall again in the dark as they had turned off the lights again. Thank goodness!

At the next doorway, I slowly opened the entryway and noticed a staircase going down. This must be it! The way to the basement! Slowly we descended the stairs, worried every second that one of the smugglers would appear either behind us or in front of us. One step at a time. We could see some light below, but it must have been a fair way off because it did not light up the stairs very well, and we almost lost our footing a few times. The stairs spiraled, and there wasn't a wall to hold onto after about the fifth step down. There was a skimpy handrail which wasn't much support in the dark. Finally, we reached the bottom. It was cement, and there were several rooms below along a hallway. We quietly crept toward the lit room, figuring that that's where the smugglers would be and Sarah. Luckily, the door was ajar, and I could see through the door's hinges.

In the room, two of the smugglers stood over by the counter where the electronic equipment was. One was Charlie. I recognized his short stature and red beard. The other was Sam. He had dark hair, a moustache and a cigarette permanently stuck to his lower lip. We held our breath as we strained to see through the narrow crack in the open doorway. We could hear the conversation between the two smugglers clearly.

"I don't know why we have to wait a week?" Charlie was saying.

"I think we have to go slow because we don't want to draw attention to it," Sam said.

"Attention! A little late for that after that trick back in Victoria, don't you think?" Charlie challenged.

"Yeah, but think of how much money we will get when it's done!" Sam was saying.

"I guess you're right, Sam, but I don't like this waiting; it makes me nervous." Charlie went on.

"And what about that brat in there, eh? What we gonna do with her?" Sam grimaced.

"I know. I think we should have left her in Victoria!" Charlie agreed in dismay.

"Are we gonna off her then?" Sam said with doubt.

"We have to, don't we? She can recognize us!" Charlie said with concern.

"Yeah, but Ted said we have to hold on to her until the deal is finished. She's our insurance, he says." Sam reassured Charlie.

"I suppose he'll ask us to do it," said Charlie uncomfortably.

"Suppose so," said Sam, resigned to the fact.

"Oh, well, we'd better check on her. She doesn't look well, and she won't eat," said Charlie.

"Maybe she'll just die and save us the trouble." Suggested Sam coldly. And with that, the two men went into the other room where Sarah was tied up.

"They're going to kill her!" Ricky said, gulping.

"I know. We've got to save her!"

"How?"

"Now's our chance," I said to Ricky, as I turned to him in the dark of the hallway. "Come on." And I slowly headed around the doorway and into the room. Ricky quickly followed. We looked around the whole room to get our bearings and find a hiding place.

"How about we hide over there?" Ricky suggested in a whisper as he pointed to a shelving unit filled with tools and boxes over in the corner of the room opposite the electronic counter.

"Good idea," I agreed as we headed toward it. Just as we reached the unit, we could hear the two smugglers coming back into the room after looking in on Sarah. We quickly ducked behind the shelves of the unit as we listened to the two men.

"I guess so, Sam, but I don't like this at all." It was Charlie talking, and he didn't sound happy about something.

"Look at it this way, Charlie, if she dies peacefully, she won't have to suffer, right?" said Sam. To that, Charlie didn't answer, and Ricky and I looked at each other in dismay, wondering if Sarah was going to be okay. I felt anger well up inside of me, but Ricky put his finger to his lip and held my clenched fist to remind me that two young boys against two grown men would not be good odds. I knew that, of course, but I just felt so frustrated and worried about Sarah that, for the first time in my life, I realized how important she was to me. Before, she was just the pain in the neck, always in the way, annoying little sister. Now she was my I've got to take care of, big brother duty, little sister. How things had changed in a few short days! What were we going to do?

We could see Charlie and Sam come back into the room. They headed toward the helmet, which stood shiny and strange, on top of the bench where the radio and the microphone sat.

"I wonder how much money we'll get from this?" queried Charlie as he picked up the helmet.

"I don't know, but I figure it's worth over a million considering what it can do!" answered Sam. "You'd better put it down before you press a button or something."

"Ah, you worry too much, Sam. I'm just curious as to how it feels on my head." Charlie laughed as he placed the helmet on his head. "How do I look, eh?"

"Get it off! You don't know what could happen!" Sam shouted as he reached for the helmet to take it from Charlie.

"Okay, okay, relax. I was only joking with you." Charlie gestured as he brushed Sam off and removed the helmet. Just then, a buzz and static could be heard on the radio, then a voice. . . . . .

- CHAPTER EIGHT -

Back Home

My mom was screaming, "Where did they go! Oh, my God!"

My dad was looking at the FBI agents with his mouth open.

"What just happened?" he wanted to know.

"Well," started Agent Dobbs, "It's not easy to explain."

"Try us!" my dad insisted in an annoyed tone.

"Well, a long time ago, at Roswell, New Mexico, an alien spacecraft crash landed. I know that the Air Force has been in denial ever since, but I'm not going to lie to you, people. You've been through too much already." My parents were dumbstruck. They stared as if they were waiting for this nightmare to end.

"Go on." My mom insisted.

"Okay, out of the crash, there were several objects of extraterrestrial origin which were stored at Area 51. About a year ago, some scientists wanted to compare some recent finds with these objects. The government would not let them go to Area 51, so instead, they shipped the objects, under military guard, to the Smithsonian Institute for study along with the other objects of recent discovery. Unfortunately, one of the guards was working for some other foreign power without us knowing it. He hijacked the shipment and took it somewhere in the Northwest. We thought maybe, Seattle because of its close proximity to Canada and the ease with which things seem to be smuggled both ways along the west coast. We have been watching both Victoria and Vancouver for a while now but were not sure where the smugglers would strike until your daughter, your son, and his friend accidentally happened upon their operation."

"Yes, I gathered most of that," said my dad in exasperation. "What I want to know is, what do those objects do?"

"Well, there is a helmet controller, which, when worn, can transport the wearer to another time and/or place," continued Agent Dobbs.

"You mean my babies are gone somewhere else, and you don't know where?" shrieked my mother.

"Yes, I'm afraid so," answered Dobbs. "But I assure you that using these devices does not harm you. That is, outside of a headache and dizzy sensation for a while."

"Well, what about that "D…D –10…" my dad started but was quickly corrected by Agent Scarlet.

"D-105, It's a homing device for the wearer of the helmet. This means that he can return to his original destination by using the button on the right of the object."

"Okay, but why did Billy and Ricky disappear when they pushed it? They didn't have the helmet on." asked my father with concern.

"Because if you are on the other side of the destination with just the D-105, it acts like a conduit to join the user to the controller of the helmet. There is also a button on the left of the D-105 which displaces time and allows you to move about invisibly due to time distortion around the holder of the device," explained Agent Scarlet.

"What was the government planning on doing with these devices? And do they have other weird things like this?" asked my mother in dismay.

"I'm sorry, ma'am, but we cannot divulge any further information due to national security." Agent Dobbs gave the expected answer.

"Humph!" my mother added. "Should have thought of that before you let it get stolen." She muttered under her breath.

"What do we do now?" my dad asked resignedly, his head in his hands.

"Well, we have some intelligence operatives in Russia and cooperation from the government there. We'll follow up on all leads and resolve this as soon as we can for you. You two need to be alert to any strange happenings or contact from your daughter, your son or his friend or even perhaps the smugglers. We have an agent set up here, Agent Scarlet, who you already know, and a direct communication link to me and the FBI should anything occur. We are doing everything we can to ensure the safety of your children. I assure you." Agent Dobbs said, looking directly at my mother, who was softly crying now and feeling frustrated and scared for us.

"I will be with you every step of the way." Agent Scarlet said with empathy in her voice as she put her arm around my mom and led her into the kitchen. My dad followed with a gaunt look on his face as if he had aged 10 years overnight. He hunched his shoulders and stared straight ahead as if in a dream. When they reached the kitchen, my mom put on the kettle for some coffee as they all expected it would be a long night.

"No, thank you," said Agent Dobbs as he explained that he had to get back to their headquarters, which they had set up downtown. He told Agent Scarlet to call his cell phone at any time and with any information, no matter how insignificant it might be. My mom, dad and Scarlet sat in the kitchen drinking coffee and wondering how long it would be until they heard something. Dad, who had studied some about UFOs, started talking about them.

"I knew there was something about that Roswell incident. I heard there were bodies found of gray beings with big heads and tiny bodies. Some of them were alive, and they took them to Area 51 and into a hangar and performed autopsies on the dead ones. I wonder if they were able to communicate with the live ones. Do you know anything about it?" he asked Scarlet.

"No, I don't know any more than rumors. No more than you, as I was not even born then. But it is interesting reading, isn't it?" she added, figuring it was better to talk about such things than to sit there and worry about the children. She was trying to keep their minds off of it.

Just then, there was a ring at the front door. Rasputin immediately did his burglar alarm thing and began to bark. Dad got up and went to answer it, expecting some unwanted salesman trying to sell them something they didn't need. He yelled to Rasputin to be quiet, and after a few more barks just for good measure, he stopped. Instead of some unwanted salesman, Dad found Professor Reynolds standing on our front porch. He looked like Sherlock Holmes in his hat and raincoat. A lit pipe extended from his lips, helping to complete the image, and he was carrying a brown leather briefcase that looked like a relic from the fifties.

"Good evening." He said as my father opened the door.

"What brings you out here?" Father questioned, as he opened the door wider to let the professor pass.

"I got to thinking about that visit your son and his friend had with me earlier, and I thought I may be able to shed some light on that artifact they brought." He explained.

"You mean the D-105?" my father questioned as he closed the door.

"I guess so. It was round with two red buttons on it that seemed to flash." Professor Reynolds remembered as he handed my father his coat and hat.

"Yes, well, come into the kitchen. We were just going to have some dinner. Would you like some?" Father offered.

"That would be nice. I skipped lunch. I got so busy today." The professor explained as he followed my dad down the hall to the kitchen. They could hear Rassy growling as they passed the basement stairs.

"Dear, you remember Professor Reynolds, don't you?" my dad introduced him.

"Of course; good evening, Professor," she responded with a smile.

"And this is Agent Scarlet. She is from the FBI." Dad continued.

"Pleased to meet you," Agent Scarlet rose to shake his hand.

"And you," he answered as he shook her hand. "This must be pretty important if the FBI is involved."

"Well, just precautions." Agent Scarlet said, not wanting to divulge too much information, to protect my mother and father.

"It's alright, Agent Scarlet. He is a trusted friend." My father reassured her. "He can know what is going on."

"In that case, can you tell me what you know of the object in question?" continued Scarlet.

"Well, I started to go through my files from a few years ago, and I found some interesting information," stated the professor as he began to open his briefcase and pull papers from it. Agent Scarlet leaned over and took great interest as she noticed that some of the sheets had a government emblem of an eagle on the letterhead, and others were stamped Top Secret.

"Where did you get those?" she demanded.

"I have friends in many places, Agent Scarlet," came the matter-of-fact answer. The professor was not shaken by her apparent accusation. "I assure you that nothing was taken illegally. In fact, one of my sources was a Five Star General." With that, Scarlet backed off, sat down and listened. My mom and dad were hanging off of his every word, hoping that it would shed some light on what was going on.

"When I looked back at my Roswell Files, I found a write-up from researchers at Area 51 that I had been given 20 years ago. It shows a picture of the same device and explains it. At this point, he raised the piece of paper he was holding and peered through his bifocals, "And I quote…

…this object which has been labeled D-105, seems to be some sort of homing device that the aliens must have used to return to their own reality. In conversations with surviving species, we have ascertained that alien beings can travel through time and space portholes by using the D-104 and D105. The D104 is a helmet-like device that, when worn, can allow the wearer to travel to anywhere that they have been. It seems to link to the thought processes of the person and identifies locations they are aware of. Then somehow, it is able to propel that person, or persons in close proximity, to that address anywhere in the known universe. This means it has to be a location already experienced. The D-105 can be kept at the previous location as a failsafe for the traveler to return or for other personnel to follow. The two devices work in tandem…"

"So, the boys are with the smugglers in Russia. We know that, but how do they get back if both devices are there!" announced my mother in frustration.

The professor looked confused, and Agent Scarlet began to explain. "The two boys who visited you and had the D-105 accidentally pressed one of the buttons and disappeared. We think that they would have traveled to where the smugglers are presumed to be, in Russia, and now both devices are there."

"Oh, my God!" whispered Professor Reynolds in disbelief as he dropped the paper and covered his mouth with his hand. "I'm so sorry. No wonder you're so upset." He turned to Scarlet. "And what is the FBI doing about it!" he demanded.

"We are doing everything we can, Professor Reynolds," Scarlet replied confidently. "We have operatives in Russia and here trying to solve this problem as we speak. The best thing that you can do is keep quiet about what you know and support Mr. and Mrs. Maclean. Let us handle the rest."

"Yes, of course," Professor Reynolds replied, "How long have they been gone?"

"Uh, about 4 hours." Mr. Maclean said, glancing at his watch.

"Well, we might as well eat," said Mrs. Maclean as she brought a salad out of the fridge and placed it on the table. She began tossing it as my dad, the professor, and Scarlet watched. They all seemed to have lost their desire to talk. When it was served, they quietly began to eat their salad, going through the motions like zombies, staring into space and all thinking, *How is this possible?* Halfway through the salad, Scarlet's cell phone went off, and they all jumped.

Scarlet pulled it out from her belt strap and pushed the talk button. "Scarlet here," she said excitedly. "That sounds encouraging……How long ago? …Where did you say?….Okay here….We're just waiting…No, just your call…Okay….Right…" She slowly brought the phone down from her face and clicked the end button. "That was Agent Dobbs. He says that our Russian operatives have picked up an unusual energy fluctuation in southern Russia, near the town of Orsk in the Ural Mountains."

"I wonder if that is where the children are?" my father said quietly as they all looked at each other.

“Are the Russian authorities going there to save our children?” asked Mom in a desperate voice.

“I’m sure they were already on their way before Agent Dobbs phoned,” reassured Scarlet. “We’ll hear something soon.”

“We’d better!” It was my father, an angry look on his face. “They’d better be okay too!”

“Maybe we should just wait and eat our dinner.” offered Professor Reynolds trying to take the worry away from my mother and father. And with that, they sat down to finish their meal, although no one felt like eating.

- CHAPTER NINE –

Out of Time

The boys froze when they heard the radio crackle.
"…A – 2 this is A – 1 …over…"
"…A – 2 this is A – 1 …over…"

Charlie and Sam looked at each other, not sure what to do. "Ted did all of the talking before. What should we do?" Charlie asked Sam.

"Well, we'd better answer, I guess. Here let me," suggested Sam. Charlie moved aside, and Sam picked up the receiver and pressed the button.
"…A – 1… this is A – 2… over…"
"…A – 2…who is this?… over…"
"…A – 1…this is Sam…over…"
"…Sam…the E30…N60…rendezvous is not going to work…area too hot…over…"
"…copy that…over…what then?… over…"
"…get ready to move to other house as heat is on the way…over…"
"…understood…what of Ted?… over…"
"…wait for him there …over and out…"
"…understood…over…"

Sam put the radio down, released the button and turned to Charlie. "We've got to get ready to move, Charlie. Start packing up all of the equipment."

"What about the girl?" asked Charlie with concern in his voice.

"We'll take her with us." Sam answered, "Now, let's get going!" With that, Charlie picked up the trunk below the bench, placed it on the bench and started to place the equipment in it. Sam grabbed equipment from the shelves to the right of us, and we ducked down just in time. They were frantically filling boxes with things, and Ricky and I both thought this would be a good time to try a rescue of Sarah. We began inching our way to the entrance of the other room where she was kept prisoner. At the doorway, hidden by the last shelf, I could see into the other room. Sarah appeared to be asleep in a bed against the back wall. There didn't appear to be anyone else in the room. I slowly slipped around the doorway until I was hidden in the room to the right of the door.

Ricky quickly followed. We dropped down beside the bed and held our breath as we waited to see if anyone had noticed us, but the two men were too busy packing things up in the other room. We peeked over the edge of the bed anxiously as we looked at Sarah. Her eyes were closed, and she looked very pale. I carefully reached over to see if she was breathing, my heart in my throat. Relief! I could feel her breath on my fingers, but it was shallow, and she seemed to be in a deep sleep. I wondered if they had drugged her.

"She's breathing, Ricky." I whispered, "But I think they may have drugged her."

Ricky looked at me, his eyes wide open. "We'll have to wake her to move her," he said quietly.

"Yeah, but let's untie her first," I suggested as I started to loosen the ropes around her arms. It wasn't easy. The knots were tight, and I had to bend down and pull on them with my teeth. Finally, after what seemed like hours, I had the rope loosened and her hands free. As I did that, Ricky had reached under the blanket that was loosely laid over her and was untying her feet. She suddenly shifted, and her eyes opened. I quickly placed my hand over her mouth and rested my finger across my lips to warn her not to speak. She shook her head and then stopped suddenly when she recognized us and began to nod her head yes. I slowly took my hand away from her mouth, and she spoke sleepily.

"How did you guys get here?" She reached out and hugged me. It felt great to give her a hug. Something I thought I would never say.

"Don't worry about that now." I told her, "We need to get out of here, but you have to be really quiet, okay?" She shook her head, yes, and we let go of each other. When we looked up, the light suddenly went on, and there were Sam and Charlie staring at us.

"How did you get here!" Sam shouted as they approached us. We jumped to our feet and held onto Sarah, who seemed very groggy still.

"Quick!" gestured Ricky, "The D-105!" I knew what he was thinking and reached into my pocket and pushed the button on the little disk. Suddenly we were in a blur with colors and that feeling of nausea welling up in our throats. I felt like I would black out, but I didn't. We were swirling through a tunnel of time and space just like before. Then, just as suddenly, we were thrown out of the vortex of color and blackness. I felt a thump under me as we landed somewhere or somewhen! Then everything went black!

- CHAPTER TEN 10 -

Back Home Again

I was dreaming in my sleep. In my dream, I could hear the ocean, and there was a bright light above me coming from a spinning saucer…a Flying Saucer…and this beam was emanating from the spaceship. It was a greenish color, and it split the night into eerie sections of black and green. Fog swirled around among the trees, adding to the ghostly scene. Where was I? Who were these intruders? Were they going to harm me? I was dazed and confused as I stood up and tried to find my bearings. Trees…Ocean…the smell of seaweed…It was like Saxe Point Park at home! I looked around, and I could just see two other dark forms lying a few meters away…Ricky and Sarah? I shook my head, and I began to hear a thrumming sound like the rotors of a helicopter. That wasn't a spaceship; it was a helicopter over the trees. And the two lumps beside me were Ricky and Sarah! We were back in Saxe Point Park!

"Ricky!" "Sarah!" I shouted as I ran toward them and began to shake them. Slowly, they rolled over and opened their eyes.

"What…what happened?" Ricky asked weakly, as he sat up and rubbed his eyes.

"Where am I?" moaned Sarah. She still seemed pretty weak from her ordeal.

"We're home! We're home!" I hugged them and Sarah began to cry.

"I want to see Mom!" she whimpered out of sheer exhaustion and relief. I helped her to her feet and reassured her that we would get home as soon as we could. We surveyed our surroundings, took a wonderful breath of sea air and looked up at the helicopter over the trees, which began circling over the parking lot in the park. We started up the path. About halfway up, we heard a terrific whooshing noise down on the beach, and a swirling vortex appeared. The suction from it disturbed the stones and driftwood, which were hurled around in a big circle. We grabbed branches and the makeshift guardrail beside the path and stared in shock. Sarah began whimpering again, and I told her it would be alright although I was not very sure of that. The vortex suddenly stopped whirling about the space, and an audible pop could be heard. My ears felt as though I had just climbed up a mountain, like the feeling you get when you take off in an airplane, and your ears need to pop to equalize the pressure. The center of the vortex went from blurry to clear as the black disappeared into regular space and time.

Then it was just like two people appeared out of nowhere. We could see that one of them was wearing what looked like a helmet. Of course, they used the alien's teleporting helmet to follow us. They lay on the beach for a moment and then began to rise. It was Sam and Charlie. They had followed us. They looked up toward the path and started moving in our direction. Sam stopped only long enough to pick up the helmet and rushed to follow Charlie.

"Quick! Let's get out of here!" Ricky shouted. He was in the lead, and we responded by rushing up the path as quickly as we could.

"There they are!" I heard Sam's voice. "Get them! They've got the D-105! We can't let them get away!" As they spoke, the two men picked up speed and hurried up the path behind us. We were terrified!

"I can hear a helicopter!" shouted Charlie.

"Hurry, before they make it to the parking lot!" exclaimed Sam. We ran fast into the trees, but they were closing. If we could only make it to the parking lot, I thought. The helicopter would be there with the men from the FBI. I was certain. I held onto Sarah's hand so tightly that she began to whimper, but I dared not let go. Just as I thought they were going to catch up, I could hear voices ahead of us. The men from the helicopter were coming down the pathway toward us. They had landed already and were coming to rescue us! We could see one of them just 10 meters away. He was carrying a rifle. When he saw us, he shouted at us, "Get down!"

We flattened ourselves against the path's roots and gravel as we heard the discharge of a gun overhead. The two smugglers were shooting at us! Then there was an exchange of gunfire between the soldiers ahead of us and the smugglers behind us. Pretty soon, the soldiers were right there looking down on us. The shooting had stopped, although one of them still had his revolver out.

"Are you kids okay?" one of them asked as he crouched down to us.

"Yes, I think so," I replied as we looked up into his face. He had a helmet on with a face shield and a microphone and was dressed in military fatigues. His gun was back in its holster, and he reached down with his hand to help us up.

"What are you kids doing here? And who were those guys?" he questioned with obvious confusion in his voice.

"It's a long story." Ricky offered. Sarah and I shook our heads, yes, and breathed out in relief. We were tired and still a little shook up by our recent encounter.

"What happened to the smugglers?" I asked at last.

"Well, after some shooting, they simply disappeared. Strangest thing. One moment they were there firing on us, and the next, there was a crack like thunder, and they disappeared into what looked like a wind tunnel. You wouldn't happen to know anything about that, would you?" He asked while removing his helmet and scratching his head.

"Well, they were smugglers, and they have a stolen device which allows them to travel anywhere by just thinking about it. It's stolen from the Smithsonian Institute, and it actually came off of one of those spaceships, you know, from Roswell, New Mexico. You know, the ones that are kept in Area 51 and…" I blurted it all out.

"Whoa. Hold on there, son. You're not making any sense. Slow down, and I might be able to understand you." the soldier reached over and put his hand on my shoulder.

"Look, is the FBI here? It might be better if we talked to them." Ricky said, trying to help.

"As a matter of fact, they're on their way. I'll take you to my chopper. You'll be safe there." he concluded as they both helped us up the path. It was still dark except for a full moon which lit up the path with a warming light. The slight summer breeze felt welcome. It was great to be back home! Sarah had a tight grip on my jacket, but it didn't bother me; in fact, it felt good to have her back with us. I don't think I will ever complain about her playing with us again.

"Are we going to see Mom?" she whined beside me.

"Yes, Sarah, everything is going to be okay now," I assured her as she hugged me while we walked. Poor Sarah, she had been through a lot in the last few days.

When we reached the parking lot, we could see the helicopter with its lights on, sitting in the middle of the lot like it belonged there. Two cars were coming down the road into the park. We stopped by the helicopter, and one of the soldiers flashed his flashlight toward the cars, which turned in alongside the big chopper and cut their engines. The back doors flew open on the first car, and our mom and dad jumped out. My mom was crying as she ran to us and hugged Sarah and me. Then, from the other car came Ricky's mom, who proceeded to hug and kiss him. Our dads were less emotional and simply hugged us.

"Good to have you two back." My dad said. Mom couldn't talk as she was still crying tears of joy and whispering, "My baby, my baby," over and over to Sarah, who was crying too.

Next, I recognized Agents Dobbs and Scarlet as well as the professor walking over. "You'll be happy to know that our Moscow operatives just called about half an hour ago and said that they have captured a man and a woman who fit the description you gave us, trying to escape Russia. They also intercepted a message about the other smugglers saying that they had gone back to their hideout. Unfortunately, by the time the Russian authorities got there, they were gone, and there was no sign of the helmet.

"Do you still have the D-105?" Agent Dobbs asked.

"I think so." I hesitated as I reached slowly into my pocket, but it was not there. "It must have fallen out when we dropped to the ground along the path."

Agent Dobbs looked at the two officers beside him, "You two stay here. Scarlet, come with me. Let Sarah stay with her mom, but I need the two boys to show me where they were." He gestured to Ricky and me then all four of us started back down the path.

"Show us where you fell to the ground, son." Agent Dobbs said as he followed us quietly. When we reached the spot where we had dropped, we couldn't see the object, so Agent Scarlet suggested we look around in the undergrowth. It was darker in the thick trees, and hard to make out objects clearly. We fanned out and kept looking. After about 10 minutes, Ricky shouted that he had found it. I rushed to him as Agent Dobbs said to be careful and not pick it up, but Ricky already had it in his hand. I tripped over a fallen branch and ran into him, jarring the D-105 out of his hand, and as he reached for it, he accidentally pressed the red button.

"Oh, no!" I shouted, but it was too late. We were instantly hurtled into the kaleidoscope of color and light as before. I felt my body being lurched forward by the intense force within the tunnel, and I couldn't see clearly above the blur of time, space and matter all around me. It is like being in some universal cereal bowl while a giant is swirling around the milk and multicolored cereal. Then, just as suddenly as it had begun, the whirlwind stopped, and all went black……

- CHAPTER ELEVEN -

Gone Again

When Ricky and I opened our eyes again, we seemed to be back in Russia, at least that's what the signpost suggested:

ORSK 10 KM

"That's one of the cities in Russia, isn't it?" Ricky asked me.

"Yes, I think so?" I responded wearily, rubbing my head after our unwanted journey.

"What do we do now?" Ricky whined.

"I don't know," I answered truthfully, feeling as about as adventurous as him at this point. "I've got to catch my bearings. Let's rest a minute."

"Me too," Ricky groaned. "There's a small shelter over by that rock." He pointed to a shabby-looking lean-to across the road from where we had landed in a field.

"Don't forget the D-105," Ricky noticed it blinking about a meter away from us on the ground. "We'll need it to get back." I nodded weakly, reached over, picked it up and stuffed it into my pocket, being careful not to press any buttons. We slowly sauntered across the field and over the road to the shelter. Once inside, we fell in a heap and promptly went to sleep.

When we awoke, it was dark, just about sunset. I could see the sun low on the horizon. "We'd better find some place to spend the night. It's getting dark." I said. Ricky and I once again began to survey our surroundings.

"Well, there is a road in front of this shack. Let's head west and see what we can find." Ricky suggested.

"Why west?" I questioned.

"Well, if we go west, we're heading toward the sun, and we might have some more light," Ricky explained.

"Okay," I said, although I really wondered if it made a difference because I think we would have to be traveling pretty fast for that to work. So, we headed west along the gravel road. It was quite pretty, with trees and meadows along the way, but after walking for about an hour, we couldn't see any houses. Then, we heard the distinct sound of an automobile engine. Afraid of who it might be, we quickly ran to a nearby clump of trees and hid. Looking out, we were surprised to see the van we remembered back in Esquimalt that we first started following from Saxe Point Park. We stepped out and decided we must have been going in the right direction after all. As we walked, we thought about what we would do.

"Why don't we just go home with the D-105 and forget this idea?" Ricky asked. "I don't want to meet up with those smugglers again!"

"Yes, but aren't you curious about where they are and what they're doing? I want to help catch them for what they did to my sister!" I reasoned.

"Yes, maybe, but I'm not Ron Weasley, and you're not Harry Potter!" Ricky argued.

"Okay, then, we're Frodo and Sam of Lord of the Rings, and we're fighting the dark forces of Mordor as we follow the evil ones in the Black Van!" I tried to sound like we were in some adventure in another world or time like "Middle Earth," but I don't think Ricky was buying it.

"This isn't Middle Earth, and we are not the characters in Lord of the Rings!" he almost shouted at me in frustration.

"Okay, point taken, but it is an interesting adventure. You must admit!" I continued to try to persuade him.

"Yes, I guess so. It is a cool adventure. Let's just be careful, okay!" Ricky finally agreed.

"Look, if you want to go back with the D-105, I'll go with you!" I turned and suggested to him, in a bit of a huff. But, before he could answer, we both saw strange lights come swirling down from the northern sky. They were different colors and seemed to pulse in a triangular shape. They also didn't seem to make any sound at all.

"What the heck is that!" Ricky shouted.

"I don't know! It looks like a UFO to me!" I added in awe.

We watched as the "ship" whirled in circles. It was like watching a Christmas ornament, except it was able to fly all over the sky. Its colors pulsed and blurred in red, green and blues. Were they putting on a show for someone? For us? We stood entranced by the beauty and mystery of it. I don't know how long it lasted, but I suddenly looked around, and the sun had set into a background of grey with orange streaks over the western hills.

Now, the "ship's" lights slowly came closer to us. We were frozen in anticipation, our eyes glued to it! As it approached, the D-105 in my pocket began to get warm. I could feel the heat through my jeans. As it got hotter, I quickly took it out to place it on the ground, but I dropped it because it was getting too hot to hold. The craft was now directly overhead. Its beautiful colored lights pulsing in a clockwise sequence- red, blue, green; red, blue, green; red, blue, green…Then they stopped rotating but still pulsed. Ricky and I tried to move but seemed frozen to the spot. As we watched, a hatch opened in the bottom of the craft between the red and blue lights and a bluish beam came out, bathing us in a warm glow. We were dumbfounded. We couldn't move but didn't feel any pain from the light. Suddenly, I felt light on my feet, and all of a sudden, I was above the ground, floating toward the ship! Ricky was right beside me, floating too. We soared up right into the disk with no effort at all, as if we had antigravity suits on. I briefly thought that this must be what astronauts feel like in space! As we floated through the hatch in the bottom of the craft, I couldn't see anything because we were looking into a bright, white light. I glanced down and saw the hatch close beneath us. Then we gently floated down to a solid surface, and I suddenly felt gravity. I felt a little nauseous and dizzy like you feel after a roller coaster ride at the fair. Looking over to Ricky, I noticed three alien creatures in front of us. They were grayish, short and had big oval eyes that were like black holes. They seemed to float above the floor of the craft. The bright lights were no longer glaring in our eyes, but I still had trouble adjusting to the dull light inside and closed my eyes for a second to get my bearings. My heart was pounding, and I was sweating profusely, although the atmosphere inside the ship seemed a little cool to my face. Ricky voiced what we were both thinking.

"Where are we?"

"I don't know, Ricky, but we're not in Kansas anymore!" I said, alluding to "The Wizard of Oz."

"Yeah, but I know how Dorothy must have felt!" Ricky quipped. Then, I sensed rather than heard one of the aliens speak to us. It was like mental telepathy. Words just jumped into my head.

"You two have traveled using a Quantum-Time Circle? At least that is the closest English words I can give it".

"You mean the D – 105?" I stammered. I reached for it in my pocket, but it wasn't there! Then I remembered dropping it as the craft came over us. As I looked up, I saw that one of the creatures with big dark eyes was holding it in his three-fingered hand. He held it in front of him as he spoke.

"Yes, it was taken from us at Roswell, where our fellow travelers met an unfortunate end. Your government has several of our technological devices plus our spacecraft in their possession."

"Area 51!" Ricky jumped into the conversation.

"Precisely. We picked you up because we need your help to retrieve the navigation helmet… Will you help us?"

"Yes, if you can take us home after we've got it back for you?" I suggested.

"As you say on Earth, *No problemo, amigo*." Ricky and I laughed nervously as we were both a little frightened by those piercing black eyes. After the last comment, I thought maybe we were in some bad horror movie and had to rub my eyes to make sure I was not imagining all this.

"How did you know about all of this?" Ricky asked.

"We have been following your race for centuries. There is very little that we do not know about you. Until you are ready to join us galactically, we must monitor your progress and make sure you are able to join your brothers in our universe. You will, one day in the future but for now, your lack of concern for your planet and fellow members of your race tells us that you are not ready. Wars, famine, cruelty, pollution, and inequities of all kinds, leave your species wanting in many areas. Someday, you will live up to your potential and take your place beside us and join our universal family".

"I wish we would smarten up and do it now! I fear some people will never learn the benefits of sharing and caring for everyone." I said with disappointment in my voice. I felt as though I were speaking for many of us who felt that way. It was like we needed to teach everyone else about basic kindness, fairness and love. It seems so simple to some of us. Why can't we just do it?

"I hear your thoughts, little one," the dark-eyed creature told me, and "you must be patient. It will happen in your lifetime." I smiled at that, and Ricky and I were not afraid anymore.

"Can we see around your ship?" Ricky asked.

"We will show you after we have received the Space-Time-Continuum device. We are about to land, so prepare to go and get the devices but be careful; these humans are treacherous."

"Okay." Ricky and I both said at the same time as we were led to two chairs by the wall of the ship. As we sat, there was a slight lurch backwards, and we stopped. It wasn't like a plane touchdown. It was quiet and hardly noticeable. I was thinking of asking why they didn't just go in and get the devices themselves when the answer came floating into my head…

"If we did that, we would disturb many lives, and the story of our intervention would cause problems with many of your kind who are not ready to know about us yet. It is better this way". Then, the hatch opened, and we were teleported out of the ship into a field. As we gathered our wits, the craft rose up swiftly and disappeared beyond some trees about 500 meters away. It did it without making a sound. All we could see were those beautiful lights around the circular shape of it.

"Let's get going," I suggested, my head still swimming a little after our encounter.

We trudged on up over the next two hills with nothing to show for it except the fact that the sun was below the horizon now, and it was getting dark. Luckily, as we gained the next rise, we could see lights coming from a farmhouse and what looked like the van in front of it, along with another car. We both started walking toward the farm, where we knew the helmet and the smugglers were. It was an easy trip, and we were crouched behind some low bushes at the back of the house in no time. As we approached the house, we were careful to use some of the surrounding trees to hide our way. We could make out two figures, both in the front by the van, so we circled the house to move toward the rear. The area was clear outside the back of the house. The gradual march toward darkness was helping to camouflage our approach. We were meters from the back door of the farmhouse now and could clearly see figures through the windows. I recognized Sam and Charlie but couldn't see Cheryl and Ted. They must be the two in the front of the house by the van. Then I remembered that they had been arrested. Who were those other two in front of the house?

We slowly snuck up to the porch. The dark now helped hide us from detection. Nobody seemed to be on guard this time. Maybe they thought that nobody knew where they were. I guess they forgot that we had the D-105. I subconsciously reached into my pocket to feel the D-105, and that's when I remembered. I had dropped it when we were taken aboard the spacecraft. And the aliens had retrieved it. I wondered why they didn't just use it. Oh well, too late to worry about it now. We carefully began to make our way toward the dark, away from the lit room. It seemed dark inside this room to the left, where we noticed a low window. We tried pushing it up, but it wouldn't budge.

"Rats, how are we going to get in there?" I grunted in frustration as I tried to lift it one more time.

"Let's try the side of the house," suggested Ricky, who was already heading up the left side along the driveway.

"Alright." I agreed, "But watch out for those two in front."

As I followed him quietly along the house, I noticed that he had come across another low window and tried opening it. This time it raised up a little.

"Give me a hand," he motioned to me, "this one is open, but it's stuck." Not seeing anyone, I moved toward him, reached up and helped him push on the old wooden window frame. It gave way a little more. The space was now about eight inches. With one more push, it moved up about 10 inches, and that would be big enough for us to slip through.

"You first, Ricky." I gestured toward the window, "Age before beauty."

He laughed and slid through fairly easily, head and one leg first, then the rest of him. I heard a slight thud and asked if he was okay. "Just peachy." He replied, "Your turn." I carefully put my hand through the space and raised my leg over the sill. Once done, it was easy to transfer the rest of my body through the opening, and I was standing on a wood floor. It was even darker than outside, and it took a moment or two for our eyes to adjust. I could see furniture in the room that was covered with cloth and a bed. Ricky had already moved over to where the inner door was and seemed to be intently listening for noise on the other side.

"Hear anything?" I whispered hoarsely.

"No, it sounds quiet." He replied in a breathy voice.

"We'd better check. Slowly open the door and take a peek." I suggested. By this time, sweat was beginning to cover me, and I could feel my heart start to beat faster.

Ricky carefully turned the doorknob on the door, and the hinges squeaked a little as the door opened. With the noise, we both looked at each other, held our breath, and Ricky stopped moving the door, afraid that someone would have heard us. We waited in silence and darkness, too frightened to move, ears trained on any noise at all. Nothing.

"Slowly open it, Ricky," I pushed to find out if we could move into the hallway. Ricky slowly opened it, and we could see nobody, so we stepped into the hall.

"Which way?" Ricky whispered.

"I don't know. Let's go to the left." I suggested cautiously.

So, with Ricky in the lead, we slowly crept down the hall toward the front of the house. Suddenly, we heard a door slam ahead of us and voices and footsteps coming our way.

“Quick! In here!” I whispered as I pulled Ricky back by his jacket and ducked into a closet off of the main hall. He closed the bi-fold door just in time as we could hear footsteps go by and the voices of two people. I guessed it was probably Charlie and Sam.

“We’d better get that helmet ready for delivery.” Sam was saying.

“They said that it was to be delivered by midnight.” Charlie stated, “And it’s 9:00 o’clock now!” That meant that they would be leaving soon with the helmet. We had to think fast. How were we going to get it out of here without them noticing?

“I guess we’d better follow them to the helmet and think about what to do when we get there,” I whispered to Ricky.

“Okay, let’s go.” He responded while opening the closet door and moving down the corridor after Charlie and Sam toward the back of the house. As we neared a corner, we heard voices again and stopped to listen.

“You go down and get the thing packed, Sam.” It was Charlie’s voice again. “And I’ll go and pack the other stuff in the van. We’re leaving in half an hour.” We were afraid of being found again, so we hurried off the way we came and hid in the closet again. Sure enough, Charlie came along and passed the closet on his way to the front of the house. When we returned to the corner at the back of the house, we peered around the wall, and the coast was clear. We could see the door to what must have been the basement. That’s where the helmet would be. We quickly gained the doorway, opened it and headed down the basement stairs. Just as we reached the bottom, someone opened the top door and turned on a light. We scurried beneath the stairs, but we had been seen.

“Hey! Come out of there!” It was Charlie shouting at us from the top of the stairs as Sam came running from the basement room.

“Where did you boys come from?” he asked as he waved a gun at us.

“Er, we followed you.” came my answer as I stuttered with fright. My heart was pounding! We were scared! He was pointing a gun at us!

"Mister, we're lost and…" Ricky started but was quickly cut off by Charlie, who had come down the stairs.

"Don't give me that! You used the D-105, didn't you?" he accused us with his gun aimed at us.

"Ye…es!" I stammered.

"Where is it then? Fork it over!" he commanded.

"We don't have it! We lost it!" I told him the truth.

"Rubbish! Now hand it over!" he looked angry as he stepped closer.

"Honest, we don't have it!" I whined, trying to convince him.

"Search them, Sam." Charlie hollered at his companion. Sam put his gun in his pocket and began patting us for concealed D-105s. When he came up empty, he shrugged and turned to Charlie.

"Nothin' on 'em." He said, and Charlie waved his gun at us and sneered.

"Well, tie them up in the laundry room. We don't have time for these silly games!"

"You heard him, boys, over there!" Sam directed as he pointed toward the room to the left of the stairs. We moved in that direction, through the door and into the laundry room. Sam came through a second later, holding duct tape in one hand and pointing toward the back wall of the small room. There was a sink, washer and drier and a drying rack.

"Put your hands behind your back!" Sam ordered. When we did, I could feel the duct tape going around my wrists. After me, Ricky's wrists were bound in the same way. "Now sit down and put your legs out!" Sam directed us. Having no other options, we complied and sat down, facing our captor. He quickly bound our legs at the ankles with duct tape as well. "There, that ought to hold ya!" Sam said and turned, opened the door, closed it and locked it. We were two stuck pigeons! What to do? We looked around for something to free ourselves with.

"We've got to hurry before they leave with the helmet!" I whispered harshly.

"I think I've found something!" Ricky squeaked as he headed toward the drying rack. "There's a nail here sticking out of this wall stud! I'm going to try and cut my tape with it!"

"Good, Ricky! Hurry!" I encouraged him as I looked around for something to help me escape. Then I saw what looked like something sharp jutting out from a bench on the other side of the room. It was a broken board with a jagged edge from the bench, which was broken in half. I crawled over to it and rubbed my taped wrists against it. It was hard to do as I kept rubbing the wood against my skin as well. Between the scratches and slivers, I was wondering if it was worth using the wood, and I began trying to pull my hands apart at the same time. Gradually I began tearing the tape a little at a time. It felt like I had been scraping away at it for hours, and my wrist hurt because of the scratches. I envisioned myself as a rat trying to gnaw through his bonds in order to make my way out of some scientist's cage in some laboratory somewhere, getting closer to freedom and the ultimate reward, the cheese, which in this case was the helmet.

All of a sudden, I heard Ricky whisper a sharp, "Yes!" and I noticed he was walking over to me, the tape dangling from his ankle. Just as he approached me, I made a final pull with my hands, and the tape around my wrists gave way. I quickly tore at the tape around my ankles and succeeded in tearing it off my pant cuffs. I stood up, and Ricky and I hugged each other in our joy of being free.

He started toward the door when I caught his arm, "Hold it, Ricky! We need to have a plan in order to get that helmet."

"Let's use one of us to distract him while the other one steals the helmet," Ricky suggested.

"Okay, you distract him, and I'll get the helmet. Then we'll take the helmet and use it to return to the aliens." I said. Ricky shook his head in agreement, and we slowly opened the door. The coast was clear. As we walked toward the other room, we could hear a sound of a car engine starting up outside. We hoped we weren't too late. We looked into the other room, but nobody was there. After a quick look around, we knew that the helmet was not there either. We hurried up the stairs and peered through the door to the upstairs hall. The way was empty of smugglers. Quickly we headed toward the front of the house and noticed the front door was open. Obviously, they hadn't left yet. We looked through a window curtain out into the front yard. We could see the van, which was backed in. It was running alright, but we couldn't tell if it was about to leave or if the helmet was already loaded. Then we saw Charlie come out of the driver's side. He was yelling at somebody still inside the house.

"Sam, hurry up! We have to get going if we're going to make that rendezvous!"

"Right down!" Sam called back from up the front stairs.

Next, we heard Charlie complaining from the far side of the van. "Slow as molasses in January. Always have to do something at the last minute!" It was Charlie. He was standing beside the van, lighting a cigarette. How were we going to get that helmet? What could we do? As I was thinking about it, Charlie began walking toward the house, complaining about Sam as he did so. We quickly ducked behind a couch in the front room and watched as he headed up the stairs with his smelly cigarette. We waited for him and his smelly habit to pass us before deciding what to do.

"Ricky, I wonder where those other two went?" I queried.

"I don't know? Maybe they were other members of the gang, and they already left?" he suggested.

"Well, I'll try and get the helmet, and you stand guard, okay?"

"Sounds good," Ricky agreed, and we both headed outside toward the van. I opened the back door and crawled inside. Ricky stood guard just in case someone came back pretty quick. It didn't take me too long to find the helmet. It was in its trunk, which was not locked this time. What luck! I reached in and pulled it out. As I held it in my hand, Ricky opened the door and said that he thought he heard Charlie coming back. I jumped out of the van, and we both raced to the left around the side of the house, but we could hear Charlie behind us yelling.

- CHAPTER TWELVE -

Home at Last

"Come back here, you little thieves!" I almost laughed at that. Smugglers calling us thieves. We could now hear Sam and Charlie yelling and chasing us. If we could just reach the fields and the woods, we could hide there. It was pitch black, and it would be almost impossible for them to find us. We ran down the first hill from the farm, which led back to the way we had come when the spaceship let us down. We could still hear the smugglers, but they didn't know which way we were going. Charlie was trying to direct Sam by yelling that we were down the hill to the east. At last, we were behind a group of trees that were nestled in a valley between the two hills that led to the field where the aliens had set us down. We stopped and hid as we saw Charlie run to our left and through the trees.

"If we stay here, they can't see us, and we're less likely to be found," I whispered to Ricky, who shook his head in agreement. As we sat there and heard the voices gradually get further away, we both looked at the helmet and thought about putting it on.

"I'll put it on, Ricky. After all, I got you into all of this, and if anything goes wrong, it should be me, not you." I reasoned.

"You sure?" Ricky said, "I don't mind doing it if you don't want to." He offered.

"No, Ricky. I have to do this." I said finally with conviction. He just watched me as I raised the helmet to my head, unsure of what to expect. He reached over and held my arm as I put it on my head. I tried hard to think of the alien's spacecraft, and I knew that Ricky was concentrating with me. All of a sudden, the woods disappeared, and the world went rainbow colors. We felt that vortex again and were swirled up into it traveling for a brief time down a tunnel. "*Wizard of Oz" time again*, I thought.

Then, as suddenly as we had left the woods, we were sitting in the alien's spaceship again. When the room stopped spinning, I removed the helmet, and our space friends were in front of us. Their strange, infinite eyes reflected the wonder in our eyes as we sat there exhausted. I felt a calming, soothing voice inside my head:

"You have done well, little ones! We will take care of you now." And with that, I began to feel my eyelids slip as I entered sleep for the first time in what seemed like ages. As I dreamed of home, my parents, my sister, Rasputin and Saxe Point Park, I felt a deep peace that I have not felt since, and I feel that I grew a lot that summer. I know that I will never be the same, and maybe one day, we'll all know how to live in peace with no smugglers, no greed, no hunger, and no war…I slept for a long time.

When I awoke, I was lying on the beach of Smuggler's Cove in Saxe Point Park. I looked around, and Ricky was lying about 2 meters away. I could hear barking and shouts from up the path out of the cove. I looked over and saw Rasputin racing toward me, closely followed by Sarah, Mom, Dad, Agent Dobbs and Agent Scarlet. Rasputin bounded up on me and began licking my face. I hugged him tight and looked over to see Ricky stand up. His parents were following closely behind the agents. His mom ran to hug him as Sarah jumped up with Rasputin and hugged me like she never had in the past. I would have told her to get lost as usual but not today. I was very happy to see everybody and to be back home! Mom was next, and then Dad. Boy! More hugs in one minute than I usually receive in a year. You'd think I'd come back from the dead or something. Although, it kind of felt like that. A lot was different. I never would hate my sister again or ignore Rasputin when he wanted his walks. I would do every chore without complaining and be home on time from now on…er, well, I would try to be home on time from now on.

"Sarah, you should've been there! There were aliens and the helmet, and we were in their spaceship and…" I spouted out, but before I could finish, Agent Dobbs interjected.

"Maybe you should tell us all about it later. When you've had a chance to catch your breath and relax with some breakfast." I hadn't even noticed, but the sun was just rising, and it was going to be a beautiful day. Breakfast sounded good, and I was extremely hungry.

"I'll make your favorite; bacon, eggs, hash browns and apple juice," Mom said cheerfully.

"Don't forget, sunny side up, Mom!" I sang back at her, and we all laughed as we headed up the path toward the parking lot. When we reached the parking lot, I called over to Ricky as he entered his parents' car. "Hey, Ricky, I'll call you later, and we can go play pirates on the beach, okay?"

"Sounds good!" he chorused back. Yes, things were going to be back to normal now. Life felt good. We piled into my dad's car, and Agents Dobbs and Scarlet followed us home. As I looked out the window, I thought I saw a shiny object circle the park and race off toward the west. I wondered if it was our friends and if I would ever meet them again. I had a funny feeling that this was not the end of this story.

About the Author

Raised in Victoria, BC, Canada, P.N. Holland (Neil) writes in memory of his wife, Kris. He has two children, five grandchildren and two dogs. Neil has taught for over 30 years in Public Schools in British Columbia and holds an M.Ed from the University of Victoria with a major in English. His writing is fast-paced, and his stories are page-turners. Neil also likes to visit schools where he shares his insights on reading and writing with students and teachers alike. Neil is currently working on another trilogy called **Mellissadorha (Vahldor** is Book One**)**, a collection of short stories and a detective series.

The Saxe Point Park Mystery is the first book in **The Vancouver Island Mysteries Series**. Neil has written a Teacher's Study Guide, which is being used to teach the novel. He is proud of the fact that his book is helping kids improve their reading and writing skills. It, and the other books in the series, **The Lost Boys of Lampson** and **The E&N Escape,** are all magical mysteries with settings close to home. Neil's books are available in softcover and ebook versions at libraries, bookstores and online (i.e. Indigo/Chapters, Amazon, Barnes & Noble).
Contact https://pnholland.com/ or https://filidhbooks.com for direct purchase options.

Don't miss out!
Visit the website below, and you can sign up to receive emails whenever P.N. Holland publishes a new book.
There's no charge and no obligation.
https://books2read.com/r/B-A-JLFK-MAKEB

www.ingramcontent.com/pod-product-compliance
Lightning Source LLC
Chambersburg PA
CBHW072012170626
46813CB00005B/2120

* 9 7 8 1 9 2 7 8 4 8 7 4 6 *